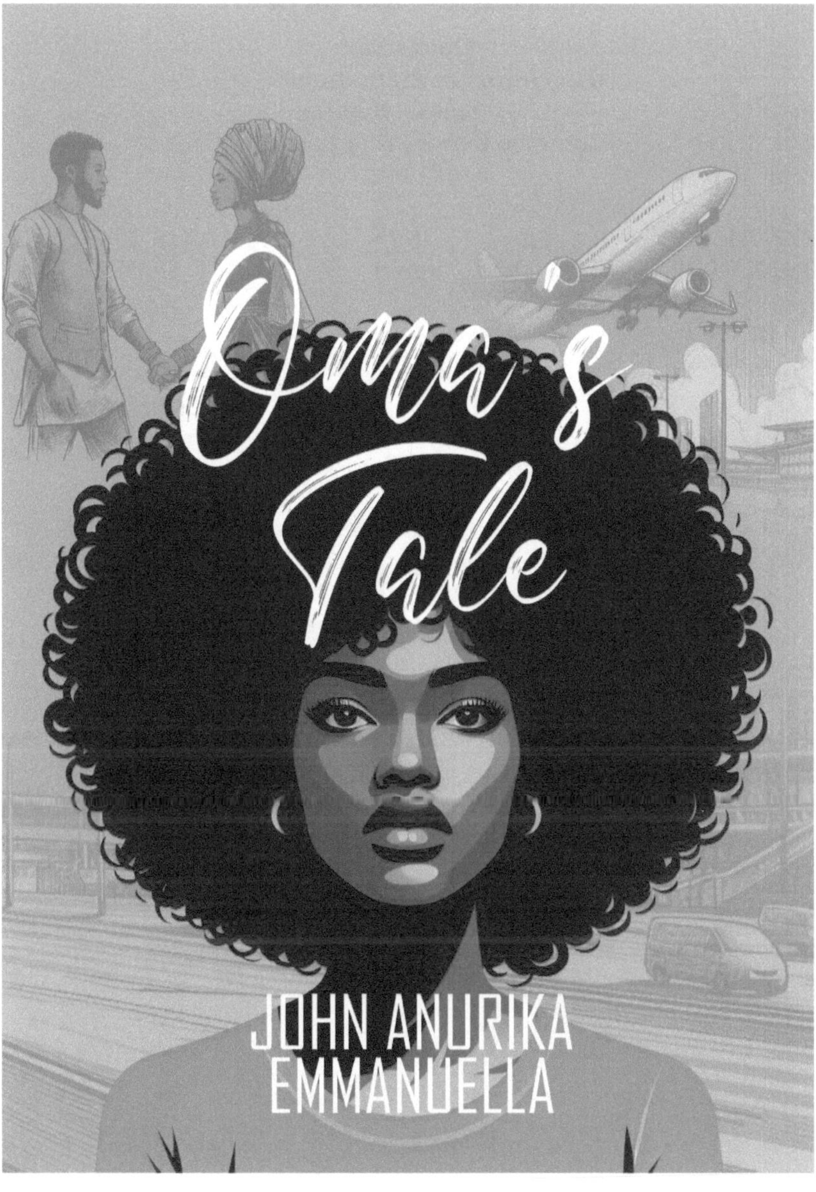

Oma's Tale

JOHN ANURIKA EMMANUELLA

NATIONAL LIBRARY OF NIGERIA CATALOGUING-IN-PUBLICATION DATA

Oma's Tale
JOHN, Anurika Emmanuella, 1995-
1.Tales—Nigeria
2.Romance fiction, Nigerian (English)
I. Title

GR351.3.J65 2024 398.209669
ISBN: 978-978-771-012-8 (pbk) AACR2

Oma's Tale

ISBN: 978-978-771-012-8

Contents

CHAPTER ONE

The tick-tock of the table clock, usually a source of annoyance, now sounded strangely soothing to my ears. I stretched and yawned, feeling like a contented infant, and thought to myself, *"What a glorious morning! What could be responsible for this radiant sunshine streaming through my window?"*

Curiosity got the better of me, and I rose from bed to investigate the day's atmosphere. As I approached the window, I was greeted by a gentle breeze and a sky that seemed to be smiling down at me - the weather was indeed perfect. Aside from the beauty of the day, something is making me happy.

"What would have made me so happy this morning? Did I win a lottery? No! Was I given a scholarship to study abroad? The answer is a resounding NO! Then what would have made me so happy?" I kept asking myself those questions.

Well, it happens to me occasionally. I just can't give a reason for my happiness this morning. I danced slowly to pick up the table clock.

"Oops! It's almost 7 a.m.," I murmured.

My happiness almost made me forget my morning routine. I had to rush down the stairs to the sitting room for the morning prayer before my mum entered my room with her loud clap and song.

I met my Mum and Dad in the sitting room, sitting close to each other. My Mum had her tambourine as usual, and Dad had his Bible. They must have been waiting for me. I greeted them, and we swung into prayer immediately.

We prayed for almost 45 minutes. Immediately after we finished praying, I already knew the next action on the line.

"Oma, my beautiful daughter, you are blessed." my Mum's usual words of advice came after the blessings. She spent almost 15 minutes talking to me. However, my cheerful disposition seemed oblivious to the passing time, and I didn't notice how long she had been talking.

When she was done talking to me, I headed to the kitchen, humming a tune as I began to tackle the pile of dirty plates. Before I knew it, I had not only finished cleaning up but also completed the rest of the household chores and even cooked breakfast. I hardly finished my house chores in time, but my happy mood must have helped with them.

As I was about to climb the stairs to my room, my Mum called me.

"Oma baby, you seem happy this morning. Can you share with me the secret of your happiness? She said this as she tickled my cheeks.

“I can’t even tell the reason for my happiness, mummy,” I replied with a smile.

“Hmm,” she said, nodding her head.

She then asked me to run an errand, delivering a message to her friend who lived on the next street. My delight wasn’t about the task itself, but about the opportunity it presented - I would get to visit Ada, my dear friend and the daughter of my mother’s close friend, and enjoy some quality time chatting and catching up with her. I dashed into the bathroom to have a cool bath. I got dressed, hurriedly ate my breakfast, and headed out to where I was sent. When I got there, I saw Ada’s Mum in the sitting room, arranging some books on the shelf. But the sweet smell and savour of some toasted bread ran through the atmosphere, which made me salivate. I greeted the woman, and she responded to my greetings with a smile.

“How have you been, my daughter?” She asked and I replied happily.

I asked after Ada and her mother pointed in the direction of the kitchen.

“Wow! So, Ada has been the one causing the spread of that sweet aroma,” I whispered.

I delivered the message to Ada’s Mum and moved towards the kitchen to meet Ada. Immediately, Ada saw me coming and began to hail me. We hugged and exchanged pleasantries. With a warm smile, she gestured to the stool, inviting me to sit and make myself comfortable, and we launched into a delightful conversation. Ada and I have been very good friends since childhood. She is the same age as me and she is very pretty. Unlike me, who only stays at home under the watchful eyes of my parents, Ada works at a television station.

Ada offered me some toasted bread. We talked about my admission, whether the admission list of the university I chose was out, and several other things until noon, then I decided to head back home while she escorted me.

My Mum, being the sweet woman she has always been, had already prepared lunch before I got home. As I entered the dining area, I saw my parents seated at the table. I approached them, exchanged warm greetings, and took my seat by pulling out the chair. With my place setting already prepared, I dug in and enjoyed the meal. Once we'd finished eating, I helped clean up by gathering the plates and taking them to the kitchen.

"Your siblings called, and they asked of you," I heard my Mum talking from the sitting room.

"Oh! Extend my greetings to them anytime they call back," I replied.

ChiSimdi and Chimaobi are my elder siblings. They are identical twins. Someone can hardly tell their difference. But the only way to identify them was their gender. ChiSimdi is a female, while Chimaobi is a male. Despite their gender, they were very close, and they did things together. I so much envy their closeness, wishing I was a twin, too. They were both in their third year at the university, but by September, they will be in their final year. I so love the twins dearly. They love me and pamper me to the extent that they never allow me to lack anything, and they will never allow even a fly to hurt me. I know I'm so blessed to have them as my elder siblings.

As I was cleaning the plates, the thought of my admission ran through my mind. BARON GOLD UNIVERSITY has been my childhood dream. It is one of the best universities in the country. I already applied to the university twice, but I wasn't admitted. Despite all that, my love for the school never ceased, and I was never discouraged. This will be the third time I'm picking the school, hoping and praying to get admitted this time around. Well, I wasn't too old, though; I finished my secondary education at a very early age.

After I had finished with the plate, I strolled back to the sitting room.

"Mum, can I make a call with your phone, please? I need to call Sis."

She looked at me and handed the phone to me. In no time, ChiSimdi picked up the call. We had a little discussion on the phone, and I asked her to help me check the school admission list, which she promised to call back after checking.

After lunch, I felt the need for a siesta. I retreated to my room, collapsed onto my bed, and let myself drift off to sleep. I was vaguely aware of my name being called, but I was too exhausted to respond. Suddenly, I felt a gentle yet firm tap on my feet, which jolted me awake. It was then that I realised my Mum had been trying to wake me, and the tap on my feet had finally succeeded in stirring me from my slumber.

"Your sister would like to speak to you," she said as she handed me the phone.

Sluggishly, I answered the call.

"Hello! Sis," I grumbled.

After a few seconds of listening, I shouted joyfully. My Mum was equally curious to know what had caused me to shout. I started jumping around my room; I moved closer to my Mum, holding her hands playfully.

"I have been given admission into Baron Gold University," I said with all my strength.

Both my Mum and I began to dance around the room. My shout made our neighbours come and ask if anything was wrong. I came downstairs and started sharing the good news with anyone who cared to listen to me.

I remembered that there was someone I hadn't informed about this news. I ran as fast as my legs could carry to Ada's house. I met her dancing as well. She ran to me immediately after she saw me.

"I have been given admission," we both chorused.

"Wow! So, has the university you chose also admitted you?" I shouted.

She responded by nodding her head in joy. We were both happy, so we rejoiced together.

I was in for a treat when I arrived home, as surprises were already waiting for me. My Dad got me a brand-new HP laptop, fulfilling his long-time promise to me if I got admission to the university. My Mum also gave me a brand-new Android phone. They must have gotten these things for a long time now, hoping to give them to me at the right time.

I was the last child of the family, and yet I was never over-pampered; they met my necessary needs at the right time, so I wasn't a spoilt child. I was happy. I hugged them both and kissed them. My joy knew no bounds. I headed straight to the small shelf in my room. I brought out the SIM pack Bro Chimaobi bought me some months ago. I inserted the SIM into my phone.

The first people I needed to call were my siblings. I called my siblings on my new phone. They were also happy for me. We had a little lengthy conversation before they excused themselves and said they needed to go to lectures.

"Hmm... I guess I know why I have been stuck with happiness since morning. This isn't daydreaming; it was all reality." I said as I lay gently on my bed, smiling.

The following week was meant for me to go and see how things were done in school. I already wrote down the necessary payments that needed to be cleared before resumption. Without wasting much time, my Dad gave me all the money for the payment, which I went and paid the following week. After making those payments, I went straight to my faculty for my registration number before I could become a bona fide student at the school.

Upon arriving at the office of the Head of my faculty, I noticed the name "Dr. Gift" prominently displayed on the door. I knocked softly, and after being invited in, I entered and greeted the woman seated behind the desk, who appeared to be in her mid-to-late 50s, busily organizing files on her table.

"You must be Dr. Gift, ma?" I asked.

"Yes, you are right; how may I help you, young lady?" she responded.

I told her my reason for coming, and she gave me my registration number. She stretched out her hand towards me.

"Congratulations, my dear! You are now a bona fide student of the faculty of Social Sciences, Baron Gold University. School resumes in September, so stay safe till then."

"Thank you so much, ma," I replied, beaming with joy as I exited her office.

In truth, "happiness" didn't even begin to describe the elation I felt.

I went home and explained to my parents how Dr. Gift seemed to be a kind woman. About an hour later, a knock came on the door; I rushed to open it. It was my siblings, ChiSimdi and Chimaobi.

"The most amazing twins are here!" I shouted happily.

We hugged each other, and they congratulated me. I was thrilled because I had my siblings around me. Being together with my siblings has always made me so happy. I have wanted to hear from Sis ChiSimdi how life in the university was because she once told me that life in the university is always challenging and fun.

After the warm welcome and cheering, everyone retired to their rooms. I went to ChiSimdi's room. I found her reclining on her bed, preparing to drift off to sleep I ran to her on the bed. She smiled as she saw me.

"Can you tell me more stories about life in the university, please, so I can fully prepare myself for whatever comes my way?" I said as I squeezed my face playfully.

ChiSimdi sat up, smiling. She began by telling me about different lecturers and their behaviour of collecting bribes and sleeping with female students.

"Though some of the lecturers are good, they don't engage themselves in such acts," she said.

She also told me about student cults and the political aspect of the university, which is the Students Union Government (SUG). She told me about several other things I needed to know about university life.

Then, she leaned in closer, holding my hands a bit more tightly. I felt a surge of positivity, and ChiSimdi's face took on a more serious look.

"You will surely become what you wish to be. If you want to be a good or bad student, it all depends on your choice. A university is a place where you have the freedom to make decisions on your own. No one will be there to stop you, not even Dad or Mum; neither I nor Chimaobi will be there with you. So, it's your choice of life," she said.

I sighed so deeply; I was moved by what she just told me.

She continued, "Oma, my beautiful sister, university life is full of fun, but do not be distracted; you must have heard about how good people become bad and how bad people become good; as I said earlier, everything is a matter of choice, so choose wisely my dear sister. I took upon myself that no matter the trials and challenges I face in this school, I will not allow anyone or circumstances to defile me, neither by sexual intercourse or bad behaviour. So, I went to God in prayers and made a covenant with Him. I asked Him to give me the grace to keep my virginity and the grace to be the best student throughout my stay in the higher institution. And God answered my prayer."

"But, sister, were your requests fully granted by God?" I asked her.

ChiSimdi sighed, stood up and moved to the water dispenser. She gulped down a glass of water.

"Yes, my requests were granted," she responded.

"I started getting distinction from my 100 level till now, and I'm fully sure my God will continue till I finish my higher education. However, challenges and temptations are everywhere. I thank God for seeing me through. So, Oma, this is all I must tell you; the ball is in your court; it's your decision and your choice," she said while lying on the bed to sleep.

It was so obvious that ChiSimdi was really feeling sleepy. I thanked her, returned to my room, and retired to bed. Within a few seconds, I dozed off. I could feel a soft touch on my face, which made me smile like a baby from my sleep. I gently opened my eyes to see ChiSimdi sitting so close to my bed, staring happily at me like a mother watching her baby.

"How time flies! My kid sister, whom I used to carry in my hands, is now an undergraduate and a big girl," she said as we laughed.

We went downstairs for the usual morning prayer and house chores. We went out, and everything felt so good and happy, just as it has always been.

CHAPTER TWO

The holiday was incredibly amazing, and before I knew it, it had come to a close. While this marked a somber return to reality for my parents, since the whole house would be silent and empty without me, but I was eager to go to school. With a mix of sadness and nostalgia, I tearfully embraced my mum in a bittersweet goodbye. The hug was tinged with melancholy, as I couldn't help but wonder when I'd have the chance to hold her close again. She gave me motherly counsel, as all mothers will do, while she tried so much not to show the tears gathering in her eyes. She then escorted me to the car that was parked at the front of our house and watched me sit comfortably in the passenger's seat.

"I will really miss my mother," I uttered silently.

After so many hours in the car, we arrived at the front of a tall, beautiful tower with an inscription on it which reads: BARON GOLD UNIVERSITY. My heart leapt for joy as the feeling of being a university student dawned on me. With a broad smile on my face, I read the words written boldly on the banner tied under the school's name, which reads, "We Baron Gold University welcome all 100 level students."

Without paying any attention to my smiling face, the driver drove right to my hostel, which was not too far from the school gate. With his masculine body shape that had been shredded due to excess labour, he helped me carry all my luggage into my room before he drove off towards the school exit gate.

My hostel was a nice, well-painted room. It was allocated to four of us. Fortunately, I came into the room before anyone else, so I picked my favourite corners. Since half of the task had been done by the driver who helped me carry my luggage into my room, I quickly arranged my corner in a very comfortable way. In no time, I was already done with the arrangement.

I then called my mum. We had a lengthy conversation as I had to describe everything I saw on the way here. After fifteen minutes on the phone, we said our goodbyes, and I slept off on my neatly arranged bed, only to be woken up by some voices after two hours. I looked up from my sleep and saw three beautiful ladies chatting happily and smiling.

These beautiful ladies must be my roommates, I thought to myself.

"Welcome," I greeted as I headed towards the bathroom for a quick bath.

Everyone would think I would join their conversation after bathing. But I went back to my bed and dozed off again.

The school's academic calendar kicked into high gear, and our lectures started without delay the very next day. I was bursting with excitement that morning, and in my haste to get to class, I forgot to fuel up with breakfast. As a result, by the time the lecture concluded, I was feeling utterly depleted. The combination of hunger, fatigue, and exhaustion was overwhelming. Thankfully, I had the foresight to stop by the refectory on my way back to the hostel, where I replenished my energy with some much-needed snacks before retreating to the comfort of my room. As usual, I met my roommates, chatting and smiling. I quickly apologised for not introducing myself or conversing with them the previous night.

"Never mind" they all chorused.

They understood that I was feeling very sleepy, and from that day, we became good friends.

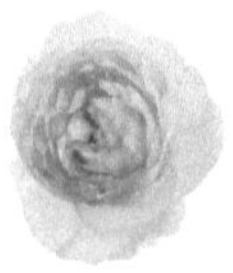

In no time, the first-semester examination was around the corner. It's already two weeks until the exam, and I've gotten used to all school activities. We started preparing for the examination. Everyone started to put in their efforts to make sure they came out with flying colours. I never relented in my studies. I began to burn the midnight candle, crushing all my notes one after the other.

The long-awaited exam came, and everyone did their best. We all prayed for the best result, which will be released a week after our exam. I really look forward to the break, which will be after the result, because I miss my Mum. A week after the exam, our results were released and pasted on departmental notice boards for all to see. You could see everyone moving up and down in search of their result. It was a great joy for me that I came out with flying colours. I had nine A's and one B, making me the best of all my courses.

My joy knew no bounds as I slid my hand into the pocket of my fitted denim pants to grab my phone. I couldn't wait to announce my achievement to my Mum and Dad, but I kept the news of me coming home the next day away from them. I wanted to make it a surprise. After dropping the call, I called ChiSimdi and Chimaobi. They were very delighted to hear my results. They also encouraged me to do better next time.

All night, I kept thinking of my parents. If I could control time, I would have fast-forwarded it so I could go home as soon as possible.

As the clock struck 7 a.m., I swiftly gathered my clothes and packed them into my bag, eager to begin my journey. With my luggage in hand, I made my way to the car park. I got home and knocked on the door. I heard my Mum's beautiful, resonant voice asking who was at the door.

"Is this the house of Mr. and Mrs. Percy?" I asked, smiling like a tickled baby at the door.

My Mum screamed for joy immediately after she opened the door. I hugged her so tightly.

"I missed you, Mum!" I screamed.

I turned to hug my Dad, who had been staring so hard at me, waiting for his own turn. We discussed my school and how hard I studied hard for my exam. My happiness increased when my Dad promised to treat me nicely at a restaurant for my excellent performance.

Once again, the whole house was lively and beautiful. We sat around the dining table, eating the sumptuous meal prepared by my Mum. I feel so happy and proud to be part of this great family. After my short break, which was full of enjoyment and pampering, I returned to school for the second semester. The semester was awesome, just like the first, as I excelled maximally in all my tests and exams.

Education for me was relatively easy because I had help from my family. During my days at the 200 level, the second semester to be precise, some group of people introduced the Chinese language learning program to us and with all the benefits they said it holds, which includes travelling out of the country to further our education, I became interested in learning the language. During my holiday, I told my parents about it and without much stress, they both agreed that I should add Chinese language learning to my education.

One fateful day, my Dad called me and told me I wouldn't be staying in the school hostel with my roommates again. This decision seemed so sudden and irrational because I'd never pictured myself living alone or living with anyone apart from Charity, Rita and Jane. Oh! I don't think I've mentioned their names before. Charity, Rita and Jane have been my roommates since my first day in school. Even though it's difficult for people to believe we live together due to their behaviour. They both love partying and flexing. So many times, they have invited me to join them, but I just couldn't because my sister's word of advice kept ringing in my head.

I disagreed with my Dad on his decision to move me to another apartment outside the school. I decided to seek advice from my sister, who explained everything. She said I wouldn't understand how detrimental my friends' behaviour could be to me. During our conversation, I realised she was the one who gave my Dad the advice to move me out of the hostel. Knowing this, I obeyed my parents, and a new, well-furnished apartment was rented for me right outside the school. The truth remains that I miss Charity, Rita and Jane, but I don't want to disobey my parents.

One of the main reasons I didn't want to change my hostel was that I hated staying alone. However, since that's inevitable, I had to find a way to cope, and with the help of my phone and computer, I was able to forget the boredom loneliness brings. My Chinese language learning classes started immediately after we resumed the 300 level. Who would have thought it would be this strenuous? Quitting wasn't an option for me because I really believe in the benefit it will surely bring, which is furthering my career abroad. This was my motivation as I combined the program with my daily school activities. Most of us in this program quit, but I was determined not to be discouraged despite how stressful it was.

"Good evening, sis. Do you have a minute? I have a few questions I'd like to ask you," my schoolmate said, catching up to me as I walked back to my apartment after a chaotic day at school.

"I'm a new student here, and I would love to hear your experience, opinion and advice," she added.

I guess she could read the curiosity on my face.

Without waiting for a reply, she continued, "I'm in the same department as yours. I've been noticing you since my first day here. I've heard a lot about you and love everything about you."

Upon hearing this, I couldn't help but burst out laughing, and she soon followed suit. I promptly apologized for not responding to her. I was astonished that someone had been noticing me, though the feeling of being praised this way felt so good.

With a broad smile, I asked, "Would you mind following me to my apartment? Because we can't have a conversation while standing."

She eagerly agreed to the offer as if she was expecting me to throw that. We both walked side by side, chatting all the way till we got to my place.

When we got to my place, I microwaved the food I had cooked before leaving for class in the morning and shared it with her. We both ate to our fill before we started our conversation. I knew I had a lot to say. Someone asking me about my school experience made me reminisce about how far I've come. I started my explanation by mentioning every detail about my 100 level days. It seemed like I was reading about my life in a journal.

"My first semester in this school was fun," I said. "I didn't have any problems to worry about until the second semester when one of our lecturers, Mr. Bartholomew, started making some love advances at me."

I could see the amazement on her face, the same we all have when we hear some moonlight tales.

"He said he would love to be my sugar daddy. He promised to take care of me and make sure I passed all my courses. He threatened to fail me if I refused his advances. Despite all his threats, I took my stand not to be subject to his offer."

"But nemesis caught up with him. One day, while we were in class, I heard a girl telling my coursemate that Mr. Bartholomew had been demoted to a junior lecturer because he was caught molesting a student. I was happy God saved me from him so fast, but a series of issues started again. Due to my academic excellence, different guys in my department started noticing me, and the advancement became too much. There isn't a single week that I won't hear the word *'I love you'* from at least three guys a week. I was determined not to date or give any of them a chance at my heart. It's apparent that none of them genuinely love me. They only want to use and dump me. However, there came a young man who seemed to be a better option among them. I started considering him and was thinking of accepting him until I discovered that he was also a Casanova!"

"What? Or who is a Casanova?" the lady asked with a curious face.

"A Casanova is a promiscuous guy who jumps from one lady to another," I answered.

"Since then, I've decided to refrain from paying any attention to any guy's word. School life isn't easy, but with God, all things are made easy. One primary reason I was able to stay focused and excel so much in this school was that I was so devoted to serving God. I go to church twice a week and on Sunday. I also joined the

Legion of Mary because I'm a Catholic, and this has really helped me in every way. I will strongly advise you to do the same, as I can see; I am sure you are also a Catholic," I added.

I could see the surprise on her face.

"But how do you know I am a Catholic?" She asked.

I pointed to the scapula around her neck, which had a picture of "Our Lady of Perpetual Help." We both laughed, and she seemed relieved.

"Pardon my manners. My name is Queen, and I'd love to be your friend so you can influence me with your good morals," she said while smiling.

I didn't bother telling her my name since she already knew.

"You're my friend already," I replied while hugging her so closely.

"I have another question, please," said Queen. "Assuming you're approached by a guy who claims to love you and would love to be your lover. But because of your level of experience, you decide to start as mere friends, and you later become lovers. After a while, he started demanding proof of love by asking for sex. What's your opinion about that Oma?"

With a concerned heart, I looked straight into her eye and said, "Queen, my dear, you're a beautiful, young, and talented girl, and I would love to see you in the future, doing so well for yourself. Don't be fooled by their sweet words, and don't misquote their infatuation for love. Tell him to come and pay your bride price if he's really interested in you, and be sure that any man that loves you will surely wait till he marries you before asking for anything."

With a smile on her face, she hugged me and thanked me. From that day on, I could feel the responsibility of mentoring someone resting so heavily on my shoulder. After a lengthy conversation that took us hours, she stood up and decided to leave. However, she promised to come to visit some other time since she now knows my place. I escorted her out of my to the main road before bidding her goodbye. It's been a while since I had such an interesting discussion with anyone.

When I got back to my room, I received some missed calls from my sister ChiSimdi. I was amazed because it's been a while since I heard her voice, so I picked up my phone to return the call. To my surprise, the twins' voices were so loud and happy; they must be together. Obviously, there is a lot of good news to share.

With a laughing and joyous voice, she shouted, "We are done with our NYSC!" she said very loudly.

I screamed at the top of my voice with joy. My twin siblings were done serving their country.

The three of us laughed aloud as we planned the future.

"The next thing for you guys now is to get a dependable job and get married to the most amazing man and woman just like you guys," I said playfully.

We all laughed so hard that we all echoed "Amen" in affirmation.

"Have you announced this great news to Mum and Dad?" I asked.

"We are planning to make it a surprise as we will be going home very soon," they both said. I wish I was present when my parents met them - it was the start of a grand celebration!

I asked them how NYSC days were, and to my amazement, I found out Chimaobi seems to enjoy the service year more than ChiSimdi. Suddenly, Chimaobi mentioned the name "Obi," and I could hear ChiSimdi hauling him. Then I realised that my sister had found true love, named Obi, the one who was ready to pay her bride price. She had been keeping it a secret from me for a very long time, only when Chimaobi let out her secret. I shouted with joy and enthusiasm.

"Why don't you want to tell me about this? He almost shared the same name with your twin brother," I said.

She smiled and said, "I was going to tell you, but it's fine since Mr. Big Mouth has made the announcement."

I couldn't hide my joy as I retreated to my bed that night; it had been one of my best nights so far.

CHAPTER THREE

Just two months after completing their National Youth Service Corps (NYSC) program, ChiSimdi and Chimaobi secured employment, courtesy of ChiSimdi's fiancé - my future brother-in-law. With their careers taking off, both families have begun making wedding preparations, and the big day was fast approaching. I also started preparing for my exams because it was near. I formed the habit of staying back in class after the day's lecture to read for more than three hours before going home. I always do it every day, excluding Saturdays and Sundays, when I study in my room.

One fateful afternoon after lectures, I stayed back to read.

"Please, can I join you?" a male voice said.

I raised my face in confusion to look at the person talking, and I saw nothing but a tall, handsome, and well-dressed gentleman standing at the door of my class. The young man noticed my confused face.

"Oh, sister, I mean, can I stay here and read?" he asked with a mild smile.

"Oh yes," I replied.

He sat down at the extreme edge of the seat, a little far from where I was. He thanked me, but I did not pay much attention to him as I concentrated more on my reading. After my normal three hours of reading, I bade him goodbye and left him in the classroom.

The next day, he also came to read and sat at the same place. But this time around, he left before me. He kept on coming to read every day. But on a particular day, he approached me.

"Hey dear, since we both read here almost every day, can I have your mobile number, just to say hi sometimes?" he said while smiling playfully.

Reluctantly, I gave him my number.

"My name is Christopher Udechukwu Karl, but my friends call me Karl, so you can call me Karl also. What's your name?" He said, still smiling like a playful baby while stretching his hand.

"I'm Omasirichi Percy. Oma is the short form of my name," I replied, also stretching my hands to meet his.

After the brief introduction, we bid each other goodbye.

From that day, we started reading and leaving the classroom together. We made some rules that would promote effective reading, such as putting our phones on silent to avoid distractions and exchanging phones, but they will be returned to the owner only if there's an important call or when we are done reading. We carried on with this rule, and it has been so helpful during our reading. On a particular Friday, after we were done reading, I decided to go to church instead of heading home straight.

As I walked home from church, I noticed a group of students gathered around the notice board. It was clear that the examination timetable had been pasted. Curious, I approached the board to check if the schedule for my department's exams was available. To my delightful surprise, I discovered that I would complete my exams well before my sister's wedding. Thrilled by this news, I strolled to my apartment with a spring in my step, basking in the pleasant breeze.

On my way, I decided to inform Karl about the timetable because I've always told him about my sister's wedding. I picked up my phone and dialled his number.

"Hello, Karl," I spoke first.

But a lady's voice answered instead of Karl. "Who are you?" The lady asked in a harsh tone. I told her my name.

"Help me tell Karl that the exam timetable is out," I said.

But the response I got sounded a little bit harsh.

"I am Karl's girlfriend. I'm also a student here, so I'm aware of the timetable. Bye."

I heard the phone click in my ear.

The whole conversation made me burst into laughter.

"Funny indeed," I whispered.

Two weeks later, we were done with the exams. I had already told Karl about my sister's wedding. He promised to come, so I gave him the address. The next day, I travelled home. The house was already full; my aunts, uncles and cousins were already at my house helping with the preparations. The whole family was so happy to see me. I saw Aunty Blessing arranging some gifts inside a big bag. I ran to hug her. Aunty Blessing is my father's younger sister, and I love her so much because she is cheerful and accommodating.

ChiSimdi had been waiting for me for a very long time. She ran to hug me immediately, dragged me to her room, and showed me her wedding gown.

"Wow!" I whispered excitedly.

The wedding gown looked so elegant and wonderful.

"This must be expensive," I shouted.

She explained that Obi, her husband-to-be, bought the gown in London. She opened her wardrobe, brought out another gown and asked me to try it on. It fits so well on me.

"You look so beautiful, Miss Chief Bride's maid," ChiSimdi said.

I was really surprised.

"So, I will be the Chief Bride's maid?" I asked.

"I was thinking of making one of my friends the bride's maid because I thought you would be busy with your exam. But I changed my mind when you told me about the progress in your examination timetable," she replied.

I was speechless. And I hugged her so tight. She started chatting about other things that made us laugh out so loud.

"Can we know the source of the laughter?" We both turned to see who was asking.

"Uncle Mikel! Bro Chimaobi!" I shouted and hugged them tightly.

Uncle Mikel is my Mum's younger brother. The two young men noticed the gown on me.

"You are looking beautiful," they both chorused.

I was so overwhelmed with joy by the compliment. Just then, we heard the car horn. Dad and Mum were back. I quickly changed my gown to something simpler and more comfortable. We all went downstairs; Mr. and Mrs. Percy looked bright and radiant. I greeted them happily.

"You must have finished your exams," my Mum said.

"Yes, ma." I replied happily.

My Mum also dragged me to her room; she showed me her clothes for the wedding and several other things. Obviously, my parents were the happiest humans on Earth.

The following day was ChiSimdi's traditional wedding, and we all became busy. No one had time to sit and chat; the chefs were cooking, and my aunts and cousins were cleaning the house. The traditional activities went so well, and it was full of fun. We all retired to bed because tomorrow was the wedding's grand finale. I slept in Simdi's room because I was already missing her.

The big day finally came. The most annoying sound woke me up: the alarm from the table clock. To my surprise, I saw ChiSimdi sitting beside me on the bed with a tray on her lap. The sweet smell of fried eggs ran through my nose.

"You made me breakfast, sister?" I asked.

My sister nodded her head with a smile.

"I don't know when I'll be able to do this again, I will miss you more, Omasirichi," she said, almost in tears.

I hugged her very tightly and started tickling her. We ran around the house playfully, and everybody envied us. We had our breakfast and had a cool bath. The makeup artist came and started some work on our faces.

After an hour, we were fully dressed. My phone rang, and it was Obi, the groom.

"Where are you guys? I'm already in the church," he said softly.

"We are on our way," I replied happily.

We took a lot of pictures before going to church. My sister was beaming with smiles.

"I believe you will find the right man today," ChiSimdi whispered into my ear.

I looked at her sheepishly. So, we headed out to the church.

Following the church service, I received a text message from Karl, stating that he was waiting for me outside. I quickly excused myself from the families and couples taking photos and made my way towards the entrance. As I caught sight of Karl from a distance, a smile spread across my face, and I quickened my pace. Upon approaching him, I noticed a tall, young, and attractive woman standing by his side.

"Hey Karl, thanks for coming," I said, smiling.

"You look beautiful and amazing," he said, holding my hands. The lady's voice cut off our greetings.

"Oma, meet my Sweetheart," Karl said, holding the young lady's waist.

"I am Sasha Kings, Karl's girlfriend. It's nice meeting you," the young lady said.

"Oh! I'm Omasirichi Percy," I responded.

"What a very young and beautiful lady, but she looked very pompous," I said to myself.

I introduced Karl and Sasha to my family. I took some pictures alone with Karl, it was obvious that Sasha wasn't comfortable with it, but who cares? After taking pictures to our satisfaction, we all left for the reception.

The wedding celebration went well and was interesting. There was a lot to drink and eat, but I was busy running errands for my brother and Mum. My brother walked up to me and whispered into my ear, "Who is that guy staring at you all day? Is he your boyfriend?" pointing to Karl.

I opened my eyes wide and shook my head in objection.

"He wasn't staring at me, and he is not my boyfriend; he is just my friend and reading mate. The lady sitting beside him is his girlfriend!" I quickly said. My brother looked at me playfully and left.

Just then, Aunty Blessing came to me; she gave me the key to Daddy's car.

"Mum said you should bring out all the souvenirs from the car," she said as she walked away slowly.

I was so tired that I walked so slowly to the car. I opened it and began to pack all the gifts.

"Can I help you?" I turned and saw Karl.

I dare not decline his help. He helped me with the items into the Hall and I made sure I packed enough gifts for him and Sasha before they left. Deep down, I was so happy to have Karl around me.

After the celebration came to an end, my sister departed for her new home with her husband.

Exhausted, I retreated to my bedroom, indulged in a refreshing bath, and collapsed onto my bed, drifting off to sleep instantly. The next morning, I woke up around 10 a.m., feeling revitalized. However, my mind kept wandering back to Karl - his words, captivating smile, and charming appearance lingered in my thoughts.

I abruptly interrupted my reverie, asking myself, *"Am I falling for Karl? Absolutely not! I refuse to entertain that idea, especially since he's already committed to someone - a rather stubborn girlfriend, at that."* I sternly reminded myself.

I went downstairs and helped clean the whole compound, and I prepared breakfast. I decided to give my sister a call.

"Hello, sweet sister" ChiSimdi sounded tired and happy on the phone.

I greeted her, and we talked about some scenarios that happened yesterday and how she got deflowered by her husband. We had other discussions as well, but we had to end the call so she could rest well.

"My sister is indeed my role model," I said silently to myself.

I resumed back to school after the long semester break. How time flies, I can't believe I'm now a finalist. I have no one to call my boyfriend; well, it's all good. On the day of my arrival, which happened to be on Friday evening, I went to church for the usual Friday evening service. While the prayer was going on, I sighted Karl in the front seat, but I pretended not to notice him. After the service, a hand dragged me, and it was Karl. We left the church together. Karl escorted me to my lodge.

"Thanks for coming to my sister's wedding," I uttered softly. Karl held my hand playfully.

"It's really fun with your family," he replied. We had a little discussion for a while, then bade each other goodbye.

"Extend my greetings to Sasha," I said. He nodded playfully as he went out of sight.

CHAPTER FOUR

The closeness between Karl and I started to increase every day as we read together. He was also fond of escorting me to my lodge after we were done reading every day. Most of the time, we go to church together after reading before he escorts me to my lodge. But I got tired of this closeness since he would only fill my ear with songs of praise of how his girlfriend, Sasha, had been so good and all.

"Who told you I'm interested in hearing all this?" I would say to myself because deep down, I was already developing feelings for him, but I decided to keep the feelings to myself.

I got so distracted and engrossed in thoughts that I thought only about Karl. But the more I thought about him, the more I felt hurt.

During one of my weekend visits to my parents, I was in my room, lost in thought that I couldn't hear my mum calling out to me from her room. She thought at first that I was sleeping, but when she got to my room, she saw me lying flat on my bed, facing the ceiling, with a single name on my lips: "Karl."

"Oma, what is wrong with you?" she shouted.

I sprang up to my feet like a bounced ball; I knew I couldn't hide anything again. I told her of my feelings for Karl and the fact that he has a girlfriend and has been singing her praises in my ears. My mum knew Karl to be my reading mate, but hearing me talk about feelings made her realise how serious I was because I had never talked to her or anyone about relationships before.

My mum sighed and sat down on my bed.

"Oma, my daughter, I know how hard this could be for you because he seems to be the first person you have ever loved, but since he's in a relationship with someone else, you should try as much as possible to get your mind off him." My mum advised me.

Her words drove me to tears as I lamented on how fate has been treating me. My mum was amazed seeing me crying because since I gained admission to Baron University, I've grown more mature and stronger. I guess this is the extreme for me.

I know how hard it will be to get Karl out of my head; he is my reading mate, and we see each other every day. My mum encouraged me and reminded me of how strong I was, which gave me the strength to stop crying. I made up my mind to get over Karl. She touched my chin, smiled, and held my hands as we both went downstairs to finish the uncompleted house chores.

I went back to school early from home on Monday so that I wouldn't be late for class. As I was about to enter my lecture hall, I heard a familiar voice calling out my name. Turning around to look at the person calling me, I saw Sasha, Karl's girlfriend, coming towards me. I never had any weird feelings since this wasn't our first conversation.

"Good morning, Oma," she said.

I replied with the same doxologies.

"I would love to discuss an important issue with you," she continued.

I was in a little bit of a hurry because I always love to be well-organised before the lecture starts, but since she insisted that the issue must be discussed on time, we moved a bit from the class.

"Oma, I hope you know that Karl and I are in a relationship?" she asked.

I replied yes, knowing this conversation wouldn't end so well with me.

"I just want to let you know that I don't joke with my man, so don't you try snatching him away from me because I've been hearing a lot of rumours about you guys. This is a warning to you: don't try anything stupid; you will go down."

Her words sent shivers down my spine, leaving me more frightened than I'd ever been before - even more than when a lecturer had once threatened to fail me.

With a shaky voice, I replied, "Sasha, I don't have anything special going on between your man and I, he is just my reading mate."

I added, "Moreover, Karl loves you so much; he talks about how much he loves you every time."

Sasha seemed not to pay much attention to what I said as she turned before altering her last word so loudly.

"Oma, my eyes are on you."

I felt so troubled that I couldn't wait for my lectures. On my way to my lodge, all I could think about was how I got myself into this mess and how to get out of it. I made up my mind strongly to get rid of any feelings I was having towards Karl immediately.

I guess Karl was expecting me to show up as usual for our reading in the evening, and when I didn't show up, he repeatedly called me, but I deliberately ignored his calls. I later had to switch off my phone when his calls were becoming too much. After one hour, I heard a knock on my door. Opening the door, I saw Karl standing handsomely and looking radiant as usual. I wasn't surprised to see him, though; my instincts told me he would come looking for me.

"Good evening," he greeted with a smile.

I pretended not to notice his look. Within a few minutes, he bombarded me with so many questions.

"What is wrong with you? Are you okay? Why aren't you answering your phone? Why aren't you reading today?"

With so much frustration, I shouted at him, asking which of the questions he wanted me to answer first. He looked so surprised to see me in such a state, and I knew I'd taken this too far. I apologised for shouting at him and told him I had not been feeling well. He touched my body to check if my temperature had changed. He also asked if I had eaten, and I said yes.

"I felt so confused and sad; who wouldn't covet such kind of care from a guy this handsome?" I thought.

I pulled myself from my thoughts. "Karl, it is getting late; you should go home now. I'll be fine, and we will read tomorrow," I said.

I could sense he felt relieved, knowing that I was perfectly fine. He turned to leave.

"Good night, dear." He said while waving his hands.

But I only replied with a smile.

In that instant, I grasped the pain of loving someone I shouldn't. Watching him leave filled me with sorrow, but I couldn't stop him. I retreated to my room, and soon, I escaped into the realm of dreams - the only place where Karl and I could be together without any obstacles.

The following morning, I woke up so late, probably because I was enjoying my dream. After my lectures for the day, I decided to read with Karl again to clear his curiosity about my well-being. Immediately, he came into the reading room; he told me he would need my help as he was preparing for a presentation in his department. Surprisingly, I never asked for his department until now when he told me he's a student of Business and Administration.

"How can I help in your preparation?" I asked.

"Just hold this copy and check out for my mistake as I go on with the presentation," he replied.

"I won't just tell you if you made a mistake, I would beat you," I said jokingly, and we both laughed in agreement.

During the presentation rehearsal, I posed some challenging questions to Karl, simulating what his lecturer might ask. Whenever he faltered, I punished him, as promised, but all in a lighthearted manner. Fortunately, Karl proved to be a bright and intelligent student, so I didn't have to "beat" him too severely. I guess that's one of the reasons why I loved him. After the presentation, I clapped for him as he came to take his seat right beside me, and then I heard footsteps approaching. It was Sasha.

"Don't bother to sit down!" she shouted as Karl was about to take his seat.

"Please, darling, my sister just called me to come over to her place, and I wouldn't love to go there alone. Would you mind escorting me there?" she asked seductively.

"As you can see, we are still reading, so please try and go alone," Karl replied.

Sasha wasn't happy about this, and with piercing eyes, she begged me to help her convince Karl, which I did. Karl was quite concerned about my safety, but I assured him that I would be alright. I pretended to be reading when Sasha kissed him right in front of me before they left.

I knew my reading had ended for that day. I was just waiting for them to leave before I embarked on the lonely journey to my lodge. It's been a while since I walked the path to my room alone; Karl was always there to escort me to the lodge.

I couldn't wait for us to finish the 400-level first-semester examination, as I was more eager to go home. I just want to leave the school environment and everything that reminds me of Karl and his girlfriend. On getting home to my parents, I was taken to the hospital because I had become so lean and sick. Deep down, I knew the cause of my weight reduction was that I'd been thinking a lot about Karl, and I couldn't wait to finish everything and leave school.

After the short semester break, and with the help of my mum, I regained my weight and prepared to go back to school for the last time. I determined in my heart to care less about Karl or anything else because I had two big exams right before me. The first was my Chinese scholarship examination, and the second was my final-year examination. On getting back to school, Karl sent me a text telling me he was sick; I still care so much about Karl, but not as much as I did before we went for a break. So, I decided to visit him after I was done arranging my room. This was my first time going to Karl's place. He described the way to his place during one of our conversations. I followed the description, and with some help from a little girl, I got to his doorstep and started knocking.

After knocking several times, he might need to be stronger to answer the door. I pushed the door, which in turn opened, but to my surprise, no one was in the room.

"Hello! Hello!" I shouted.

I heard a familiar voice from a small room, which I guessed was the bedroom.

"Oma, what are you doing here? Why disturb our peace? Does this place look like a reading room?" Sasha asked furiously.

I was so ashamed of myself.

"Karl sent me a text that he was not feeling too well, and I'm only here to check on him..."

Just as I was about to complete my sentence, Karl came out of the same room wearing shorts, asking who it was before he saw me.

"Oma, you're here," he said.

"I received your text message saying you were not feeling so well, but with the look of things, I guess you are now fine, so I will take my leave now," I replied.

"Oh, such good reading mate. Thanks for coming," Sasha said sarcastically.

She turned to kiss Karl, but he pushed her away and reached out for my hand, telling me not to mind what I saw.

"I just finished bathing; that's why you are seeing me like this," he tried explaining.

"Why would you need to give me any explanation?" I asked.

"After all, this is your house and your girlfriend, so you're free to do anything you want." I added with a smile, but deep inside me, I was boiling with anger and there was an angry look on Sasha's face.

"Get well soon and be fine," I said as I forcefully released my hand from his grasp and headed out of his room.

As I headed home, my mind was flooded with thoughts, and I couldn't shake off the regret of visiting him. The image of her, kissing him, made my stomach turn. I was dismayed to realise I still harbored feelings for him. The next day, Karl and I met at our normal reading place, but immediately he came around. He tried explaining what happened in his house the latter night, but I wasn't interested in his discussion. I asked about his health and what the sickness was precisely. He said he was diagnosed of malaria and typhoid, but he is getting better as he used the medication he was given in the hospital. I asked him to go home to rest, but he insisted on staying because he wanted us to go to church together. This seemed to be a good reason, though, so I focused on my reading and only heard him call my name after some minutes.

"When is your scholarship examination? And if you get the scholarship, will you truly leave for China? He asked.

"The exam is this month; passing my exam and leaving this country is my goal, so I will definitely go if I'm given the scholarship," I replied.

His expression changed, and he looked so sad.

"What's wrong," I asked him.

"Oh, nothing, it's fine," he replied while replacing the expression with a smile.

After my hours of reading, Karl and I both moved down to the church. But all through the service, I noticed he was staring so hard at me. I became uncomfortable with this and warned him to stop, but he didn't stop until we finished the service. As everyone was leaving for their various hostels, Karl asked if he could escort me to my lodge as usual, but I bluntly objected. He insisted, but I gave a loud shout that could bring tears to the face of a toddler. He felt terrible and apologised before turning back.

I also felt so bad about this, but I don't regret what I've done. I hurriedly moved through the path to my lodge with a mixture of anger and sadness in my heart. I got to my lodge, and while I was trying to open my door, I sensed that someone was staring at me, but I couldn't see the person. Since Karl was the only guy who loved staring at me that hard, I had no issue assuming he was the one standing somewhere to make sure I was safe. I smiled and retreated into my room for the night.

After some weeks of reading and preparation, the day of my scholarship examination came. I wrote the exam with much confidence. While waiting for my result, I had to prepare for my second exam, which was my last examination at Baron Gold University. Due to exam preparation, Karl and I became closer, and this can be misinterpreted as something else, as we spent more time reading and chatting than before. I also noticed he stopped singing the praises of his girlfriend; this was quite a relief for me as we found some other things to talk about. Meanwhile, my feelings for him grew every day.

Finally, I finished my exam. What a relief after four years of studying! But I still had one more thing to take care of, which was my project defence.

One week after my school examination, while preparing for my project, I got a message on my phone that read, *"You have been awarded a scholarship to further your education in China. Congratulations."* I jumped up and screamed for joy because my long-awaited dream had just come true.

I tried calling Karl to inform him about the scholarship, but I remember he had travelled home to his parents since he had finished his examination and project. I texted him to call me whenever he was available, which he did some minutes later. I asked him when he would be back because I didn't want to share the news on the phone. He gave me a date that coincidentally turned out to be my project defence day. I invited him to meet me directly at the defence hall, as I couldn't wait to share the good news with him in person. I hadn't expected to see him so soon, but I suppose that's what happens when you're feeling happy and excited - time seems to fly by.

After my defence that day, I felt so happy because I had prepared so well before going for it. Right after the defence, I picked my materials to leave the hall in search of Karl, whom I expected to be around by that time, but as I stepped outside the hall, I noticed two strong men wearing black-coloured shirts moving so fast towards me and another one from the opposite side. I couldn't make much sense of the scenario until I saw one of them so close to me with a knife. I had given up hope of being saved by any angel because they were too close to me, *"What can I do against three strong guys?"* I thought.

The next thing I heard was a splash and a firm, masculine hand holding me so tight, but I didn't feel any pain in my body. Opening my eyes, I saw Karl right in front of me, holding his back with his white shirt all stained with blood; then the whole scenario became clearer. Karl saw those guys trying to harm me, and he rushed between me and the guy holding the knife, who in turn stabbed him before they all ran from the scene.

With tears in my eyes, I shouted for help, and all the students rushed around to help Karl, who was now lying unconscious on the ground. We rushed him to the hospital as I reminisced on how bad the day had turned.

"Who wants me dead?" I asked myself countless times.

CHAPTER FIVE

Right behind the car of the good Samaritan who helped us to the hospital, I felt the pain of those who had lost their loved ones and how devastating the whole process would be. The kind of heartbreak they were subjected to, but right in my heart, I prayed to God for mercy to save the man I secretly loved. We got to the hospital, and the nurses wheeled him on a stretcher quickly into the emergency ward. They tucked him gently into an empty bed where the doctor attended to him. We were all assured that he would be fine, and in the last two hours, I felt like I just took a new breath. I requested for his phone, which was later given to me by one of the nurses, then I called his parents and Sasha, who later ran down to the hospital.

After speaking to the doctor, Karl's parents came to me, and Sasha introduced me to them as their son's reading mate. I couldn't interpret the expression on their faces; all I knew was that it wasn't so friendly. Sasha hugged me.

"Come outside; I want to have a word with you," she whispered into my ears.

"Karl's parents said you should stay away from their son after hearing the cause of their son's accident," Sasha said.

This word sank deep into my heart. But I summoned the courage to ask what they had heard about the incident.

With a sharp and loud voice, Sasha replied, "You think I haven't asked around? I knew the attackers came for you but stabbed Karl while he was trying to save you, and I already told his parents everything."

Tears welled in my eyes, and I shouted, "What do you think is the cause of all this?

"If you truly love yourself, stay away from Karl unless you want to see the wrath of his parents," she added before leaving for the ward.

After my discussion with Sasha, I never bothered going inside. I went to my lodge in tears and felt devastated. A lot of bad thoughts kept running through my mind, and I felt I was going insane.

I knew I needed to speak to someone. The only person I could talk to right now was my Mum, so I picked up my phone and called her number.

"Mum, what if he dies? What if I won't be able to see him again? What if I've made a mistake by not telling him how much I love him?" I said sadly on the phone.

After a long chain of questions, I was relaxed. I explained everything that happened, including the fact that the knife was aimed at me.

"Did you offend anyone?" My Mum shouted furiously.

"I've never exchanged words with anyone, neither have I fought anyone," I replied faintly.

Thinking about the fact that someone was trying to kill me was a mystery on its own, but I'm not so concerned about that right now; all my focus is on Karl. My Mum was so worried. She told me to be home this evening unfailingly. I genuinely do not want to leave Karl all alone at the hospital, but I also must go home for my safety.

The next day, I arrived home looking pale. My Mum was so worried about me. She tried her best to make me comfortable, but my mind was on Karl.

"How is he now? Is he fine? I hope the pain isn't severe." I kept thinking about him! After so much thinking, my body could no longer hold the pain. I began to doze, but the sound from my phone woke me up. It was a nurse from the hospital where Karl was admitted. I had collected the nurse's mobile number before leaving the hospital so I could find out about Karl's welfare.

"Karl is in coma," the nurse said.

I did not allow her to say the next statement before I hurriedly got up from bed. I took some money from my drawer and headed out. I met my Mum in the kitchen, picking beans. I hurriedly explained everything to her and dashed out.

I got to the hospital in no time. I could not find both Sasha and Karl's parents; I guessed they must have left. But still, I perceived I wouldn't be able to enter the ward where Karl was. A hefty man was standing at the front of the door. I knew the man was there, so I wouldn't have access to see Karl. I went back to the nurse, who dressed me up like a nurse so I could enter the room without anyone stopping me. Nurse Yemi had been so kind to me since I brought Karl to the hospital.

"Thank you so much, ma," I said as tears of gratitude rolled down my cheeks.

"I understand your feelings, dear; I was once in your shoes," she said.

I rushed straight to where Karl was. Fortunately, the hefty man wasn't there again.

"Where would he have gone?" I thought. But who cares? I entered quietly and locked the door behind me.

I saw Karl lying unconsciously on the bed. I could only hear the beep of the machine standing so close to him. I could not help but shed tears uncontrollably. I went closer to him and sat down on the bed, holding his hand. He looked peaceful with his eyes closed tightly.

"Karl, you are so amazing and loving. I just can't understand why all this is happening. I can't imagine sharing the news about my scholarship when you are here on the sick bed. I just hope you can hear me now," I whispered.

"I got the scholarship, and I will be travelling to China earlier than expected. But there is something I really wish to let you know before leaving; I love you so much, Karl. I realised late, but keeping it for a very long time was the mistake I've ever made." I said as I shed hot tears.

"I'm sorry, this will be the last time we will be together. I'm moving very far from you. I can't deny the fact that I put you in such a bad state. Please fight so hard for your life. You mustn't die; I've always known you to be strong. I'm sorry that I won't be here to see you open your eyes, and I won't be here to bring you flowers. I've come to say goodbye, but my heart will forever be with you." I added mournfully.

I gave him a peck on his cheeks and left the ward. I saw the hefty man returning, maybe from the toilet, who knows. He could not stop me, thinking I was a nurse. I went back to Nurse Yemi, gave her the uniform, thanked her, and left for my lodge. When I got to my room, I packed some of the things I knew I could carry without stress, leaving the rest for my Mum and driver to carry. I travelled back home the following day.

At home, I explained everything to my Mum. She consoled me like a baby. I must say, I have the best family ever.

I prepared all the things I would need for my stay in China. Two days before leaving, I went to my sister's place.

The day I was leaving, my family members escorted me to the airport. As usual, I received advice from both my sister and Mum. I boarded the plane, and we took off. The thought of Karl kept running through my mind—how loving he is, our smiling days, fighting days, and most especially, how he encouraged me not to quit learning the Chinese language.

"Karl has all the qualities I want in a man; he is a good husband and father, but we are not meant for each other. Sasha is the lucky one here, and I pray she holds him tight." I said to myself quietly as I dozed off in my seat.

We arrived in Ethiopia and boarded another flight to China, which took us more than 18 hours.

"What a far distance from Karl and my family," I whispered.

I got to China safely. A cab had already been waiting for me at the airport. The cab drove straight to the apartment that was allocated to me.

CHAPTER SIX

"I am Mrs. Li, but you can call me Mama if you wish," she said with a bright smile on her face.

"My name is Omasirichi Percy. You can call me Oma," I responded with a smile, too.

Mrs. Li is the mother chosen for me in China, and immediately after I saw her, China felt like home.

Can I give you a Chinese name? she asked.

I nodded happily.

"Yes, you can."

"So, I will call you Feifei," she said and hugged me passionately.

I met Mrs. Li in an apartment; she is the guardian who was appointed to me. She is very kind and passionate. She took me in and showed me my room. The whole house was well-decorated, and my room was decorated just the way I wanted it. It had a feminine appearance. My bed sheet was pink, and almost everything was pink.

"Hope you like the room?" she asked.

"Yes, Mama, it's precisely the way I love it. But how do you know I love this colour? I said as I stared at the beautiful paintings and decorations on the wall.

"The apartment was decorated based on what was filled in your form; that's why we always ask for your favourite so we can make you feel at home."

"Ohhh.... that's true, thanks a lot," I said and hugged her, and she left.

I moved around the room, still admiring the nice wall decoration. I freshened up and went downstairs to join Mama in the dining room.

"Your food is delicious, Mama," I said.

Mama just looked at me and smiled. The pronunciation of "Mama" wasn't my usual dialect, nor was it in English; it was in the Chinese tone.

When I was done eating, I collected her phone to call my parents because I hadn't informed them of my arrival in China. They were very happy, and we also had a lengthy discussion. I ended the call, and in no time, I slept like a newborn baby. I was tossing around the bed as I opened my eyes peacefully. My eyes went straight to the tickling wall clock.

"7 a.m.?" I whispered to myself. I couldn't believe I didn't wake up from my sleep all through the night, although I had a stressful day.

I slowly got up and made my way to the bathroom, where I brushed my teeth, used the restroom, and washed my face. After freshening up, I returned to my room, said my prayers, and then set out to find Mrs. Li. I checked her room, but she wasn't there, so I decided to look for her downstairs. She wasn't in the sitting room either, and as I was about to check outside, I paused at the entrance of a nearby room, intrigued by the commotion coming from within.

I saw Mr.s Li on the treadmill, sweating profusely. I was surprised at what she was doing. She must have been exercising for more than an hour, I thought to myself. At first, she did not notice my presence until I coughed, and then she stopped.

"Oh, Oma, Good morning. How long have you been standing there? She asked.

"It has been a while since I did that. Can I join you, Mama?" I asked.

"Of course, you can, but I won't be staying much longer because I have to prepare before going out," she replied.

I joined her to exercise. Mrs. Li was never tired of the exercise, unlike me. I stopped to take some rest every 10 minutes. I don't exercise during my stay in school; the only exercise I do is rushing to class whenever I was late. We exercised for thirty minutes. Mrs. Li gave me some things to do, then prepared and left. I did all she asked me to do. Since I had nothing else to do, I went to sleep again.

When I woke up, Mama was staring at me. "Welcome, Mama; when did you come back?" I said as I sat up properly on the bed.

"It has been long since I came and also long enough to hear you are calling Karl even in your sleep," she said while smiling.

"What! I've been mentioning Karl in my sleep?" I asked her amazingly.

"Yes, my darling, you did, and I know Karl must be a special person to you, so tell me about Karl; who is he?" she replied sarcastically. Mama, please, I won't want to talk about him now. Let's leave it for some other time," I said, tears almost dropping from my eyes.

She sighed deeply. "It's fine if that is what you want, my dear; go and freshen up. We are going out," she said as she walked out of my room.

I couldn't help but ponder why Karl's name kept slipping out, even in my sleep. Shaking off the thought, I got out of bed and changed into a suitable outfit for our tour. We visited the Beijing Opera, where we were treated to a captivating performance of traditional Chinese dance and other exciting acts. The venue showcased a diverse array of Chinese dance styles and stunning costumes, we had so much fun before leaving for home.

We got home very late and tired, so Mama and I retired to bed after bidding each other good night. She also promised to take me to some historical places in China the next day. I woke up with tears in my eyes. I checked the time, and it was just 2 a.m. I saw Karl in my dream. Each time I sleep and wake up, I do not remember what we were doing in the dream; the only thing I see is tears, and this has been occurring since the day I came to China.

In the morning, after the usual chores, Mama and I sat on the couch, having some discussions. Mama told me some Chinese histories that our teachers back home didn't tell us; I was glad she did because I would be spending two whole years in China without going back to my home country. So, I needed to know some history of the place I would be staying in for two full years.

Later that day, I bought a new SIM card, which was connected to my laptop. I communicated with my parents via Skype. Mama and my parents spoke too; my parents thanked her for her kindness towards me because I had already told them how she gave me a warm welcome and made me feel at home. Three months later, I have gotten used to lectures, home, and the surroundings. I go out to school on my own, come back, and do things myself, and sometimes, I drive Mama's car to school when she does not go out with it.

My mother unexpectedly called me one weekend while I was chatting with Mama on the balcony. She said she had some news for me from home and asked me to log on to Skype. I eagerly connected to her online.

"Guess what, Oma," she said.

I frowned playfully.

"Mum, you're making me nervous, and you know I'm not good at guessing," I replied.

My Mum then changed her speech to the Igbo dialect.

"Karl has fully recovered," she said.

I adjusted myself on my bed. "How did you know, mummy?" I asked her hurriedly.

"He left here not too long ago. He pleaded with me to give him your China address, but I refused. He even said he went to your lodge but did not see you, and he had to sleep there, thinking that your lodge mates were lying to him. It was until the caretaker opened the door for him and he saw that nothing was in your room; he then believed and had to come to the house. But despite all his explanations, I still did not give him your address; I just told him to go. I guess he really needs to see you," My Mum said.

I was so happy that Karl had recovered. I've been feeling guilty that I wasn't there to stay with him at the hospital, and he was in that position all because of me. I also knew he would come looking for me.

"Thank you for not giving him my number and address," I replied.

"Oma dear, I know how much you love Karl. Even the blind can see it, but please don't think about him; you just need to forget him," my Mum said.

"Ok, ma...thank you so much, Mummy. That's why I will always love you," I said with a smile on my face.

My Mum really understands me; she listens to whatever my plight may be. I asked after my siblings and Dad, and she told me they were all doing fine. We had other discussions until I ran out of data. That is my Mum for you. She won't stop changing topics during discussions. I know very well that she misses me so much, and I miss her too. A month later, I decided to call Karl to check up on him since my Mum informed me of his recovery. Although I tried not to give a thought to it, I couldn't take my mind off him. At least I will hear his voice after a very long time.

His phone rang, and someone picked it up.

"Hello, good morning"! I said softly.

"Good morning," I heard a female voice instead of Karl's voice. It's Sasha's voice, I said to myself.

"I would like to speak to Karl," I said.

"Go ahead. I am his wife. You can tell me whatever you want to say to him."

Wife? Is Karl married? A lot of questions popped into my mind. I spoke Chinese to cover up, and I cut the call. I could not control the tears that were flowing from my eyes. So, I can't have him to myself any longer? Did he really love Sasha? I began to ask myself different questions, but I couldn't find answers to any of those questions.

Mama came to my room and saw me crying.

"What is the problem, Oma?" She asked while sitting close to me.

"Karl is married, Mama," I said with so much tears as I hugged her tightly.

"Who is Karl?" she asked.

I told her everything about Karl and what transpired between us.

"Hmm," she sighed heavily.

"Stop crying, dear; now you know he is married, so it is high time you move on. I know how much you love him because I've caught you several times talking to his pictures each time you got a good grade, and I know how you won't stop calling his name even in your sleep. But you have to keep whatever brings about memories of him," she said while patting my back.

"Ok, Mama. It's difficult, but I will try; I have no other choice," I said, moving closer to her.

Still crying, she placed my head on her lap and made me sleep. After I woke up from my sleep, Mama and I went out. She took me to some calm places that were refreshing. We did not leave the place till midnight. I went to school the following day, but my mood was filled with melancholy and downcast. I was very sad that I had to sit on the last seat in the class. Even as lectures were going on, all I could think of was Karl. I did not know when the lecturer left the class because my mind was totally far from the activities going on around me.

A tap on my shoulder brought me back to reality.

"Feifei, are you alright?" a masculine voice said while standing beside me.

"Yes, I'm fine." I responded.

"You've been like this since morning, and I am sure you did not know when the lecturer left the class," the guy said, looking worried.

"Just thinking about something, but I am fine now," I replied hurriedly.

I stood up to go home, but he followed me.

"Feifei, I know of a cool place you will love. Can we go there together now?" He asked me as he followed me.

"No, I'm not interested, thanks," I replied.

"I insist, Oma," he said.

I stopped and looked at him, surprisingly. "How did you know my real name?" I asked him.

"I've been watching you since the day you stepped your feet into the school, and I will be happy to be your friend. My name is Dawei, but I like it when people call mc Terry," he said as he stretched his hands to me.

"Wow, that's amazing; I'd like to be your friend too," I said, stretching my hand at his hand.

We went to a cool garden opposite our school. We discussed my unhappy mood. I really needed to express my feelings to someone who was willing to listen, so I told him everything about Karl. Terry was hilarious. I laughed so hard at his jokes. He created a funny atmosphere that made me forget my worries about Karl. After so much fun, he escorted me home, and this became our usual routine. He started doing things that Karl was doing when we were still in school.

Mama once told me to make use of Terry to get over Karl.

"He is a good man, and I think he will make a good husband." She often said that to me, but all I would do was laugh.

Indeed, Mama was right. Terry is a good guy, but I've decided not to have a relationship with him or anyone else until I finish my program in China. Terry continued to be the good guy. He was always there whenever I needed him, and we became closer.

CHAPTER SEVEN

Terry and I became closer, not because I loved him but because I took him as a friend, although he is a good friend. He picked me up from home to school and also dropped me home after school. We read together and we were always in the same place together.

Two years later, I was done with my program in China. Fortunately, I got a job in one of the Chinese companies there. So, I go to work in the morning and come back in the evening. And I've been enjoying my usual routine. Terry also got a job, but it was very demanding. He was swamped and very busy, and we see each other only on weekends.

My parents were thrilled and very happy when I told them I was through with the Chinese program. But they were a little sad when I told them I got a job in China and I wouldn't be coming home earlier than expected.

I know so well that they are missing me. But I assured them that I won't be working for long.

"Come back to Nigeria and look for a good man to marry; don't marry a Chinese man!" This was my mum's usual statement whenever we were on the phone. But I've always believed that I will end up with a good man when the right time comes.

I ride in Mama's car to work most days because she doesn't go out very often. We've become close; I know everything about Mama, and she knows everything about me. We shared things and attended family occasions together. She took me in as her daughter. She would usually introduce me to people as her adopted daughter.

Even on the night I had my graduation party, she threw a surprise party for me. I came home very tired, only to find the whole house very dark. Suddenly, the lights came on, and I could see a beautifully decorated sitting room, different pictures of Mama and me hung on the wall, and a giant cake placed on the table.

I heard a loud shout and clapping as Mama's family members came out to celebrate with me. We hugged and partied all night. I was overjoyed. Every one of Mama's family members was amazing. But there was something that saddened me, and that was Karl. How I wish he was with me. I came home from work very late. I retired to my room, but thoughts of Karl filled my mind. I sighted Karl's picture, which I always placed by the small bedside shelf. I held the picture and stared at it; I didn't know when the tears started rolling down my cheeks.

"Karl, I hope you're fine wherever you are. I miss you so much, but I just have to let go. You've missed a lot of my stories because I have a lot to tell you. I have finished the race you motivated me to start, but I wish you were here to celebrate my success with me." I was saying all these, not knowing that Mama had been watching me.

Immediately I sighted her, I rubbed off my tears with the back of my hand so she wouldn't notice my tears.

"I saw you, Oma. You can't hide this from me," she said as she moved closer to me and patted my back like a baby.

She then sang me a lullaby in Chinese. I was overwhelmed with tears until I fell asleep.

The following day, I went to work late because Mama decided not to wake me. After my usual working activities, as I was about to head home, I got a phone call from Terry saying that he would love me to escort him to the airport the following day to receive his cousin who was coming to China. So, I quickly added that to my schedule for tomorrow.

The next day, in the afternoon, I didn't go to work because it was a weekend. Terry came to pick me from home, and we left for the airport to pick up his cousin. At the airport, we stood waiting for Terry's cousin, and suddenly, someone tapped me on my shoulder. I turned to check who the person was, but my eyes saw someone I had never expected to see in China after two years. The person was putting on a blue jacket and black pair jean trousers with a pair of black sneakers, looking beautiful as usual, wearing a sunshade.

"Sasha!" I whispered to myself.

"Hello, Omasirichi. It's been a long time. Long time no see, sweetheart," she said, smiling sarcastically.

"It has been a while, Sasha. What have you come to do in China?" I asked

"I've come to China to see you, Omasirichi," she replied

I was shocked at what she said. I couldn't believe my ears.

"Why will you leave Nigeria to come look for me in China?" I asked.

She laughed aloud.

"Well, it might sound funny because you weren't expecting me, but I tell you, coming to China for you isn't a joke. Karl is here in China to look for you," she said.

"Ka...Kar...Karl is in China?" I asked, stammering

"Yeah, but thanks to my lucky self, I found you first. If you don't want what happened in Nigeria to repeat itself, stay away from Karl because you won't escape the nemesis of disobedience this time around."

"What is she talking about?" I thought to myself

"I don't know what you are talking about. I have nothing to do with Karl, not before, not now, and not ever; this is my guy," I said, pointing to Terry.

Sasha laughed softly and moved closer to me.

"Omasirichi, a word is enough for the wise," she whispered to my ears and left.

I was so shocked that I could not move my feet from a spot. Terry noticed my mood; he took my hand. Just then, they announced the arrival of his cousin's flight.

We picked her up and left for their house. My mind was not at rest; I wasn't concentrating at all. I went outside to receive fresh air, but my mind kept pondering on what Sasha said at the airport.

What does she mean by I won't escape from her this time? Did she send those men to kill me? And why would Karl come to China for me? All these questions kept going through my mind. I couldn't wait any longer at Terry's place. I headed home and called my mum immediately. I told her what had happened between Sasha and me. She told me to be more careful.

When Mama came back, I also narrated everything to her and pleaded with her not to let Karl come to the house. But she told me that her niece called to tell her that she gave our address to a young man who kept begging for it, and his name was Karl Ude. My heart skipped at that. I pleaded with Mama to tell him that I had relocated to a new place whenever he came. Since I heard that Karl was in China, I started waiting until nightfall before coming back home from work. I hardly went out on weekends so that I wouldn't bump into him, and sometimes, I would call Mama to know if he was coming, so I wouldn't show up.

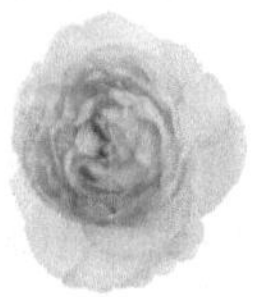

One fateful weekend, I went to the market to buy foodstuffs for the week; as I was moving closer to the fishmonger to buy some fish, I saw Karl also pricing some fishes, but he did not see me. As soon as I sighted him, I covered my face with my face cap and adjusted my hair till he passed beside me.

"Thank God he did not see me," I said, sighing.

That was when I became very sure of what Sasha said about Karl being in China.

When I got back from the market, Mama told me that Karl had come to the house looking for me.

"Eh!" I shouted.

"What did you tell him?" I asked.

"He asked if you live here. I said you don't," she replied.

"Thank you, Mama," I responded, hugging her tightly before entering my room.

I didn't know what to think about precisely, I didn't really know what I wanted. I didn't know if I really wanted to see Karl or not. I wasn't sure if indeed I wanted Karl to leave me alone or if I should be happy that he was here in China.

The next day in the afternoon, I decided to talk to Terry about it. I called him, and we met at our usual spot. I told Terry what had happened, and he was surprised.

"So, what do you intend to do next?" he asked.

"I don't know, but I don't want Karl to see me, that's all," I replied.

"Hmmm....he won't see you, alright?" He said.

I nodded my head in affirmation. We had lunch and headed to our respective work place.

Since that day, Terry had formed the habit of taking me home after work because of Karl, and I appreciate it. He had become more caring than before. Although he was always busy at work, he didn't pick me up in the morning because he usually left earlier than me.

I knew so well that Terry loved me, but I just couldn't love him the same way he did. I tried forcing myself to love him, but it just didn't work.

My love for Karl never died. And because Karl is in China, there is a high probability of seeing him around, and I don't know how I would react if I saw him. Will I be happy, sad or angry at him?

I've never told him how much I love him; he was not even aware of my feelings toward him. I became so confused. Several thoughts came rolling through my mind every day.

I was at work when Mama called in the afternoon, informing me that Karl had arrived at our residence, to look for me. On this occasion, he entered the sitting room, where he observed my personal items and pictures on the wall.

"But why did you allow him inside?" I said almost angrily.

"Feifei, you need to see how he was begging me, and I had no choice but to let him in," Mama replied.

"But trust me, dear, I told him that you left after completing your studies," she added.

I sighed heavily.

"Where is Karl now?" I asked.

"He left already," she replied.

I thanked her and ended the call.

My mind became clouded with Karl's thoughts. I could not concentrate anymore.

After work, I waited for Terry to come and pick me up as usual. Instead of taking me home, I asked him to take me to our usual cool spot. We had so much fun; at least I felt so relieved from my thoughts for good two hours. It was already getting late, so we decided to go home.

Terry drove the car slowly to the compound. I got down gently from the car and turned to enter the house when a sweet voice called my name.

"Omasirichi Percy," a voice I recognised said.

I stopped immediately. I know that voice; I can recognise that voice even in my dreams. It's Karl. I raised my face only to see Karl standing behind me. I was shocked because he was the last person I was expecting to see that night. A lump formed in my throat as tears began to gather in my eyes, but I summoned all my willpower to hold them back. Karl's gentle approach, his hand extended in a comforting gesture, only made my emotions more turbulent. I instinctively shifted away, creating a small but significant gap between us, as if trying to shield myself from the intensity of the moment. Terry came down from his car, ignoring Karl; he held me by my hand and took me inside. I guess he must have been observing the scene. He took me to my room and left.

Mama came knocking on my door, but I refused to open it. She left unhappy. All through the night, I thought about Karl until I slept off. I woke up the following morning, prepared for work and had my breakfast. I picked up my bag, bade Mama goodbye and opened the door to leave. But surprisingly, I saw Karl standing at the front of the door. Did he come here that early? Or did he sleep here? I kept asking myself. I tried walking past him, but he grabbed me by my waist and kissed me. Immediately, I forced myself out of his embrace and slapped him.

"I'm sorry. This is what I've promised myself to do whenever I first set my eyes on you again, but I wasn't opportune to do that yesterday," he said.

I didn't utter any word; I was trying so hard to hold back my tears.

Terry showed up to give me a ride, and I jumped in without hesitation, even though I wasn't expecting him since he doesn't normally pick me up in the mornings. As we pulled out, we drove right past Karl.

I was a mess of emotions - happy that Karl kissed me, but also regretful for slapping him. The kiss brought back all the good times we shared, and my feelings for him intensified. The whole day was a drag, and the weather didn't help, making everything feel grey and chilly. I felt terrible about what I did, and the thought of going home and facing Karl made me nervous. Terry came as usual to pick me up, and we went home together.

Again, I saw Karl standing at the front of the door. Terry came down from the car to open the door for me. As I got out of the car, Karl moved closer to me, looking tired and weak.

"Oma, please, we need to talk privately," he said, looking pale.

"As you can see, I just came back from work, and I'm tired. So, we do that some other time," I said, walking in with Terry.

I served Terry some tea because of the cold weather. Terry left, and I retired to my room.

Not quite long after, Mama entered my room. And she sat down on the bed beside me.

"Oma, can you just try to listen to Karl? Do you know that he slept outside all night yesterday? And he is likely to do that again," Mama said. I opened my mouth in shock.

"He slept outside in the cold all through the night?" I asked. Mama nodded her head in affirmation.

"What will be will be, and no one can stop it if you both are meant for each other. Please hear him out. Although I once told you to forget about him, I'm seeing something different now. I pray God directs you in the way to follow," she added.

She did not wait for me to say anything; she left my room after giving me a peck on my right cheek. I kept pondering on what she said till I slept off.

I felt a hand caressing my body like a baby. I gently opened my eyes to see Karl, who was staring at me lovingly.

"Good morning, Oma," he said softly.

I sat up gently.

"Karl," I whispered gently.

"I'm here to confirm if what you really told me in the hospital when I was stabbed was true. Or maybe I was just imagining you talking to me," he said as he held my hands calmly.

I couldn't say anything, but tears started flowing down my eyes.

He continued, "I wasn't in a coma; the doctor, who happens to be my cousin, brought out the idea. During those times, I only wanted to confirm if you love me. I know what I want now, and all I want is you."

"So, you weren't in a coma then?" I asked, looking weird because I was surprised.

"Yes, I wasn't," he said.

I got up from the bed angrily and went towards the door in tears, but Karl rushed to me and held me closer to himself.

I struggled to let go of myself from him, but he held me so tightly and kissed me so passionately.

I stopped struggling and I kissed him too. We kissed for long. He gently withdrew his lips from mine and hugged me so warmly.

"I'm so sorry, Oma; I wanted to tell you how much I love you, but it happened to be the day I got stabbed, so I couldn't tell you anymore. And I searched for you when I recovered. I didn't know I wouldn't see you after you left the hospital," he said, almost in tears.

"But you're married," I said.

He released me from the hugs and looked into my eyes, surprisingly.

"Married? When was I married? To who? Where? He poured out all these questions at a time.

I told him what happened the day I made the decision to call him and how Sasha answered the phone, telling me that he was married.

"Oma, I'm not married to Sasha; it is you I truly love, and I want you to give me the chance to express it. I only came to China for one reason, and the reason is you," he said, holding my cheeks in his hands.

I hugged him with tears flowing down my cheeks.

"Promise you will never leave me again. I thought I would not see you again, and that pierced my heart so deeply." I said.

"I promise to love you with all my life and never to leave you again, Omasirichi Percy," he said softly. We kissed again, even longer than in the earlier one. We decided to have fun outside the house, and Karl took me out on a date.

When we got back home, I saw Mama arranging some old books on the shelf properly. Karl entered the sitting room, smiling at her. She was amazed to see us together, smiling and holding hands. I explained the whole scenario to her and how I decided to give love a chance. She was so happy that she danced round the sitting room.

"Nothing will ever put asunder between you two," she said.

"Amen," we both chorused.

Mama prepared us some food, and we ate together. Karl and I went to the sitting room to discuss.

Later that day, I received a call from my Mum. I opened up to her about everything that was going on with Karl and me. She was happy for me, but also cautioned me to be more careful. We chatted about various things, and I asked her to extend my greetings to Dad, my siblings and my cousin, even though I had seen them during their last visit to China for a holiday.

I went back to Karl, and we continued our discussion. I told him about all my experiences in China so far. I asked him about his relationship with Sasha.

"Sasha was always angry whenever I mentioned your name because I couldn't stop thinking about you. She knows how much I love you. I caught her cheating on me with one of the company workers, so I had to use that as an excuse to quit the relationship," he said.

I laid happily on his lap, staring into his handsome face. He kissed me on my lips and on my forehead. We watched movies together until we both slept off on the couch.

CHAPTER EIGHT

The following day, after breakfast, Karl prepared and arranged his lodge. He has been unstable since he came to China. Since he had accomplished his mission of winning back my heart, he had to go home to arrange everywhere. But we won't stop seeing every day. He dropped me off at work and came to pick me up after work. Sometimes, we had dinner together before he left for his house.

The next day at work, I received a call from Terry that he would like to discuss something with me. During lunchtime, I waited for him at the restaurant opposite my workplace. Not quite long ago, Terry came in with a young and beautiful lady whom he introduced to me as his girlfriend.

"Oma, when I realised how much you love Karl and that it's obvious you don't love me, I decided to find love elsewhere. Please, meet my girlfriend," he said, holding the young lady by her hand.

I became so happy about it.

"I am Omasirichi Percy," I said, stretching out my hands to the lady.

"Oma..ric...hi..ris.." The lady tried to pronounce my name, and I burst into laughter.

"Never mind, just call me Oma then," I said.

"Ok, I am Jamila Khan, and it's nice to meet you finally. Terry talked a lot about how amazing you are; he also told me everything that had happened to you and how you are back together with the man you love. I wish you luck, dear," she said, smiling.

"Thank you so much, Jamila. I appreciate it, and I also wish you luck with Terry. He is a good guy with all the qualities a woman wants. I will say you are lucky to have him, and please, Jamila, take good care of him for me," I replied.

Terry's face was beaming with smiles as he quietly listened to our conversations.

I faced Terry, "I'm thrilled that you got the most beautiful woman in the world; thanks so much for your support and understanding," I said, hugging him.

"You're an angel sent to me by God, and I appreciate all you do. From now on, I have a best friend," he said.

We chatted for a while and went back to our respective places of work. Karl came after work and took me home.

Karl had made it a daily routine to pick me up from work every evening. Although he couldn't drop me off in the mornings due to his earlier work schedule, he would constantly apologize for not being able to do so. On that particular Friday evening, Karl arrived at my workplace to collect me as usual. As we drove home, we engaged in a lively conversation, enjoying each other's company in the car.

"Have you gone around China?" I asked.

"No, I haven't," he replied.

"So, you haven't been to the Great Wall of China?" I asked again.

"No, I haven't, but what do you know about the Great Wall of China?" Karl asked.

"The Great Wall of China is the longest in the world. The wall spans from China's western frontier to the east coast, totalling around 5,000km (3,100 miles), but the most integrated and best-preserved sections are close to Beijing," I said.

"Wow, my baby is now a citizen of China," he said, tickling my cheeks.

"Have you also been to the Forbidden City in Beijing?" I asked again.

"Of course, your answer will be capital No," I added.

He laughed hard.

"Of course, you're right. I've not been there before, but can you tell me about that too?" He said.

"The Forbidden City in Beijing is a place where we have over 8,000 rooms with golden roofs that were elegantly designed and painted in red and yellow," I said.

"I haven't gone to those places you mentioned because my first mission here in China was to win back my angel. Now that I have her and she has been to almost everywhere in China, she must take me to those places," he said, and we both burst into laughter.

He planted a kiss on my forehead, and we planned to visit some Chinese tourist centres every weekend. We decided to visit some places in China this weekend. On

Saturday, I took Karl to the Great Wall of China. Karl was amazed at what he saw, and I was also amazed when I first saw it. We spent a lot of time there, taking pictures and having fun. We also visited the Forbidden City in Beijing, where we spent an hour.

We went to the Li River in Guilin, a watery wonder with a waterfall. The surroundings were awesome, and we had so much fun there, too. We played games and did other lovely activities until evening when we left for home.

The next day, which was on Sunday, he came to pick me up in the afternoon to continue our tour around some Chinese tourist centres. We went to the ocean park and then visited the Beijing Zoo, where we saw different kinds of animals. As I bought some ice cream from a shop in the zoo park, I saw someone that looked like Sasha, but I was not so sure of it because she covered herself with a veil so that I couldn't see her face so clearly. I tried to move closer to the lady, but she turned and left. I wasn't bothered about it, though. I went to meet Karl, who was waiting for me to bring the ice cream.

We snapped many pictures, and Karl did not stop pulling me close to himself, kissing me from time to time. People around kept staring at us because of the way Karl was playing around with me.

"They are the best couple I've ever seen so far." I overheard a woman saying that to her friend.

I was happy and prayed that Karl and I would end up happily together.

Karl embodies all the qualities that women adore in a partner. He is a romantic at heart, loving, and caring, with a compassionate nature that makes him empathize deeply with others. His gentle spirit and aversion to causing harm make it rare for him to intentionally hurt someone. Although he seldom gets angry, when he does, his emotions can be intense, and his actions unpredictable. However, he has a remarkable ability to manage his temper, often choosing to walk away from situations or people that provoke him, rather than letting his anger escalate into something regrettable.

The weekend was so beautiful that I wished the day would not end, but it had to end for another day to begin. Karl took me home. We went inside the house; we saw Mama folding some clothes in the basket; she looked happy and bright when she saw us.

"I have already blessed your union," she said to us.

Karl and I laughed.

"Oh, Mama, what makes you think we will end up together?" I asked sarcastically.

I could feel Karl's reaction as he looked at me very closely, expressing his disapproval of my statement. He stood up facing me, "Please don't joke with things like this, or else you want me to have a cardiac arrest," he said, squeezing his lips playfully. We all burst into laughter. Karl spent more time with us, and he left for his house.

Work continued as usual. Karl kept taking me home after work, so I decided to ask him what kind of work he was into.

"What work are you into precisely, baby?" I asked during one of our rides home.

"I work with a Chinese company in Nigeria; I was sent to come and learn some techniques from the company's headquarters here in China," he replied.

"Hmm," I nodded. "That's good; they must have seen some great qualities in you before you could be sent here to China to learn. I'm proud of you," I said. He smiled at me.

The following weekend, we continued our tour to some Chinese tourist centres. We travelled to Hong Kong and lodged at the Bride Tea House Hotel; what a wonderful place! The next day, we went to the Hong Kong Tramway (Ding Ding), where we had an amazing ride. We also visited Hong Kong Park and the Hong Kong Stadium. We bought some ice cream from a vendor and padded to the Guizhou Huang-wushu waterfall. I love the waterfall. We spent a lot of time at the waterfall, watching it rise and fall gracefully with a splash on the rocks below.

Karl just kept on looking at me lovingly. "I never knew you love nature this much," he said.

"Now you know," I replied, smiling back at him.

CHAPTER NINE

We left the waterfall in the evening, though I wished that we stayed longer. We went back to the hotel, packed our things, and we travelled back to Beijing that same night. Throughout the whole journey, Karl kept staring so hard at me, but I never complained because I was enjoying it. Deep down in me, I wanted more than a stare. When we arrived at my house, we said our goodbyes to one another.

As I was about to go in, Karl said, "Oma, come here."

I turned to look at his face again, wondering what he wanted to say that he couldn't say during our stay at the hotel. But instead of speaking, he moved closer and wrapped his arms around my waist. The moment his hands made contact with my skin, it felt like my entire world had been turned upside down, leaving me breathless and disoriented.

I remembered how a part of me really wished he had made love to me in the hotel last night while the other part prayed he doesn't try to because if he tries to, I won't resist him.

"Is everything alright?" I asked while he held on to me,

"Yes, I just wanted to let you know how much I love you," he replied.

He raised my head, and he placed his lips on mine. This sent a shiver down my spine, and I could feel my heart pounding so hard that it was trying to come out of my chest.

He released my waist and whispered to my ear, "Goodnight, Oma," and turned to go.

I stared so hard till he ran out of my sight before I went inside my house.

I could feel great joy in me as I lay down on my bed, thinking of Karl.

Karl is a romantic guy that every lady would want to have. I'm sure that no lady can resist his kisses because he's very good at it. Terry is also a good kisser but not as good as Karl, not because I love Karl, but from what I saw, I can say who's better. I slept off that night without taking a shower, only to be woken up the next day by my alarm.

"It's Monday morning again," I groaned.

I quickly rushed out of bed to prepare for work, cooked breakfast and ate with Mama before leaving for work. Time went by so fast, maybe because I was anticipating the evening when I'd see my love again, but unfortunately, he called me to say that he wouldn't be around to pick me up because he was going to deliver his project.

On my way out of the office, I saw Terry.

"Are you done for the day?" He asked me.

"Yes, I'm done," I replied. He offered to take me home, but I told him to take me to our usual spot because it'd been a while since I'd been there. At our usual spot, we discussed many things, including his relationship. He told me how well his girlfriend, Jamila, has been treating him.

"Jamila is a very good girl, but to be sincere, I've not seen a girl like you, Oma. I feel sad that I don't have you, but I thank God for you because He gave you the perfect man," he added. I couldn't say anything as he talked.

After spending the evening with Terry, he took me home and asked me to call him anytime Karl didn't have a chance to come pick me up after work. He hugged me and left. I watched him leave.

When he was out of sight, I turned to enter my house and saw a letter dropped at the door. I picked it up and entered the house. I dropped my bag on the couch in the sitting room.

I opened the letter, and to my amazement, I saw an inscription in it, **"BE WARNED AND STAY AWAY."** All the words were written in block letters. I couldn't comprehend the meaning of the message; I just dropped the letter on the table and went upstairs. When Mama came back, I showed her the letter, but she only asked me to be careful.

The next day, when Karl came to pick me up from work, I showed him the letter.

"This might be a mistake, and it doesn't mean anything. So don't worry about it, sweetheart," he said, and I nodded my head, feeling soothed and calmer.

I was not bothered about the letter until the person sent it a second time. This time, I saw it on my desk. I asked the company's messenger if he knew the person who had delivered the letter, but he only said a little boy had brought it. The letter was the same as the first one. I called Terry and asked him to meet me during lunch.

During lunch, I told Terry about the letters. His response got me scared.

"Well, you don't have enemies here in China. I don't know who might be doing it, but you just have to be careful from now on," he said.

"How else do you want me to be careful?" I asked.

"Just make sure you don't stay out late all by yourself," he replied.

After the discussion, Terry left for his office, and I went back to mine. I became so bothered about the letter for the rest of the day.

Three weeks later, things continued the way they used to be. I forgot about the letter, and I concentrated more on my work and relationship with Karl. I didn't bother to tell my Mum about the letter because she would become so worried. I also wanted to avoid her talk about coming back home and getting a husband.

I went to work the following day, although I didn't really feel like going out. I had no choice and couldn't stay back since I haven't established my own company that would allow me to work when I wished and rest when I needed to.

Karl called me and told me he would be travelling to Hong Kong today and would not be back until Friday. I was at work till 9 p.m. because I decided to do the remaining work my boss gave me, and I didn't want to take them home. My colleagues had left, so I was the only one left in my office. I was still working when it started raining. I called Terry to find out if he could come pick me up. But his response didn't seem certain.

I checked the time, and it was 10 p.m. It was quite late, and when I noticed that the rain wasn't falling heavily anymore, I packed my things and decided to go. I sent Terry a text not to come again. I went outside and stood by the roadside, looking for a cab. I was holding an umbrella, and suddenly, I saw a bright light coming from the right direction; the light shone so brightly that I couldn't see, but I kept on waving, hoping it might be a cab. Suddenly, I felt a heavy push. I fell to the ground, and as I turned, I saw Terry. He stood up immediately and asked me to follow him.

On our way home, I asked him what the push was all about.

"You were almost run over by a car, and you didn't even know!" he said, panting heavily as he drove away very fast.

"Sincerely, I don't understand all that happened," I replied.

"Sasha drove the car," Terry said.

I dropped dead on my seat.

"Sasha?" I whispered fearfully.

CHAPTER TEN

Mama was already worried because I had never come back this late; she knew I didn't like staying late outside, so she did not go to bed; she waited for me in the sitting room. When she heard the sound of the car, she hurriedly came outside. She drew nearer to me and asked, "Oma, why did you stay late out there? Is anything wrong with you?" She looked so worried.

I didn't reply to her questions, but rather, I took her inside the sitting room. Terry parked the car we drove in and followed us into the house.

"Mama, I almost got killed by a running car, but Terry came to my rescue," I said.

She became so scared.

"Who would have done that, my dear?" She asked, holding my hands tightly.

"Sasha!" Terry said.

"Isn't she the lady you told me about who was threatening you when you were in Nigeria?" Mama asked.

I nodded my head in affirmation.

"But why would she want to hurt you?" Mama asked, looking at me even more worried.

"Well, Mama, the last time we saw Sasha was at the airport. She warned Oma to stay away from Karl, or she would not escape what she would do to her the next time. But thanks to God, I came to the scene earlier to rescue her. If not, she would have been in the hospital now." Terry said.

"I'm so grateful to you, Terry, for saving her life," Mama said.

Terry stood up, bade us goodnight and left.

"Why would Sasha say you stole Karl from her? And I believe she won't stop trying to hurt you unless you leave Karl. I guess there's more to this," Mama said.

"Sasha is just nothing but an asshole," I said, looking tired.

"Have you told Karl about it?" Mama asked.

"No. Karl is not in town for now. He went on a business trip, but he will be back in two days," I said.

"Please tell Terry to pick you up from work till Karl comes back," Mama said.

I knew that's the best option, but I don't just want to inconvenience Terry.

"I will be fine, Mama. Please, you don't have to worry too much about me," I said, hugging her and then I laid on her lap to sleep.

"It's been a long time since you sang me a lullaby. Please sing for me," I said.

Mama smiled at me. She began to sing till I slept off.

I suddenly woke up from my sleep. It was a bad dream. I prayed and slept back again on Mama's lap; she was asleep too.

On Friday morning, Karl rushed into my office. I was surprised at the way he entered.

"Oma, are you alright? He asked, touching my face, looking worried.

"How did you know?" I asked

"Terry told me what happened, so I decided to see you first before any other thing," he replied.

"Where did you see Terry?" I asked.

"Don't ask me that, he blurted out impatiently. Just answer my question!" he said, looking very worried.

"I'm perfectly fine. Terry saved me," I replied.

Karl had a deep breath of relief and hugged me so tightly.

"Please, I don't want to lose you, and I think it's time we start making plans on how to go back to Nigeria. Since you have already worked for one year, your company can now transfer you to their branch in Nigeria." He said.

"I applied for a transfer to the company's branch in Nigeria a month ago, so I'm waiting for my letter of transfer. But one of my colleagues said it will be approved in two months' time," I replied.

"That's a brilliant idea, dear," he said as he raised my head to kiss me, but I withdrew.

"This is my office, and I don't kiss in my office," I said while smiling.

He laughed slightly.

"Okay, ma, as your lordship, please," he said, taking a bow.

I laughed at the polite gesture.

He sat on the chair in front of me and was staring at me.

"Why have you been staring at me?" I asked.

"Just admiring your beauty," he said.

I smiled sheepishly.

"How was your business trip to Hong Kong? I believe you succeeded in all you went there to do," I asked quietly.

"Yes, I did, and like you, I will be done in the next two months, so we will both be free to go back to Nigeria and start working there."

Karl's presence in my life became almost ubiquitous as he began spending virtually all his time with me. His devotion to my safety was evident in the way he would wait for me at the restaurant opposite my office during work hours, his eyes scanning the surroundings with a mix of protectiveness and affection. He would take me to and from work every day, a routine that continued unabated for an entire week. However, beneath the surface of this seemingly idyllic arrangement, I harboured growing concerns. Karl's decision to abandon his work commitments had far-reaching implications, not just for his own well-being but also for our relationship and our future together. During our ride home after work, I decided to bring up the issue.

"Karl, I want you to start work, please, dear. I will be fine. I don't think Sasha is that bad. She only did what she did to scare me," I said.

"Oma, there is nothing you will say that will make me change my mind. I won't stop picking you up from home, to work and from work to home. I will keep on staying around you till I'm sure of your safety. And please accept this, my lady," He replied.

I didn't bother repeating anything. The Karl I knew cannot be convinced by mere words but by actions. When we got home, I went inside the house without saying goodnight to him.

The following day, he was at my door to take me to work again. I refused to enter his car but instead insisted I take a cab to work. I did the same thing after work. This got him so angry, but he refused to show it.

When Karl arrived at my house, he found Mama in the sitting room, engrossed in a YouTube video. He requested that she call me downstairs. As I entered the room, I could see that Karl was visibly furious - his anger was palpable and evident in his body language.

"Karl, I've told you that I want to be alone. I can go to work on my own and come back. You can always come to pick me up, but not staying around my workplace all day long. You don't even go to work, and that is what I won't accept." I said angrily

"Oma, I have told you, your safety is what matters more to me. I don't care about my work," he said in a soft voice.

I guess he was trying not to get angry at me.

"But I do care about your work, Karl. If you don't stop what you are doing, you better not come to pick me up because I will not enter your car," I said.

But he only left without saying anything to me. Mama came down from her room and moved closer to me.

"I think Karl is right. Your safety is all that matters right now; you should listen to him and don't be stubborn, my dear," Mama said.

"But he has a job to do! He works for a company that doesn't belong to him. He will be taken as an unserious fellow, and Mama, I'm so sorry. I won't change my mind on this," I said and left for my room.

The next day, Karl stubbornly came to pick me up, but I did not enter his car. Instead, I took Mama's car and went to the office. He still waited for me at the restaurant, and this annoyed me. When I was done for the day, I went to him angrily. He stood up and looked at me without saying a word. He entered his car and zoomed off.

People were staring at us, but I didn't care. I entered Mama's car and started the engine, but it wouldn't work. I tried it several times but to no avail.

I went and opened the bonnet to check what was wrong with the car, but I couldn't point out what exactly was wrong. I hit the battery with a little stone, but the car refused to start.

I became disturbed and walked towards the other side of the car to call one of my colleagues at work to find out if she had a mechanic's number who could fix the car.

The next thing I could remember was that I became very weak. I lay unconsciously on the floor. Blood gushed out of my nose and mouth and from a deep wound in my stomach. I was hit by a car coming towards me at a high speed. People around me called an ambulance, and I was rushed to the hospital. One of my colleagues who witnessed the incident contacted Mama, Karl, and Terry.

Karl got to the hospital first. Some minutes later, Mama and Terry arrived. Mama had been crying from home when she heard the news. I was rushed to the emergency room, and the doctors and nurses were running up and down; they were all busy doing one thing or the other, trying to resuscitate me.

Karl was looking at me through the open glass on the emergency room door, tears in his eyes.

"I shouldn't have left her; I told her not to be stubborn; I told her to let me guide her and that her safety matters a lot, but she would not listen," he said angrily to himself; he was crying like a child.

Mama was also crying, but Terry was consoling her.

Not quite long, the doctor came out. They both rushed towards him

"Please, who can I speak to concerning Miss Percy?" The doctor asked.

"Just talk to us. Is she alright?" Terry replied

"Hmmm.... she has lost consciousness and also lost a lot of blood. So the only thing you have to do is to pray she survives." The doctor said.

Both Terry, Mama, and Karl stood in shock.

Karl rushed inside the room, but the nurses pushed him out. He struggled to enter, but they would not allow him.

"Oma, please don't do this to me," he said with tears in his eyes.

A nurse approached Karl.

"If I were you, I would rather go to the hospital chapel to pray than stand here crying," she said and left.

Karl went to where Mama and Terry were standing. He then told them that he was going to the chapel. Mama also followed him.

At the chapel, Mama went on her knees and prayed profusely. Karl knelt in front of the altar where Jesus' crucifix was.

"Lord, you know how much I love her. I don't want her to die. Please give her another chance to live, and I promise we will go and get married on your altar. God, please grant me this favour I ask of You," he said and bowed his head while crying.

Not quite long after, Karl got a call from Terry that he should quickly return to the ward. Karl rushed back, forgetting that he had come with Mama.

When he got to my ward, the doctor came out to them. "Thank your God, she has regained consciousness, but don't stop praying till she is fully recovered," the doctor said.

"Can I see her now?" Karl asked.

"Yes, but don't disturb her," the doctor replied.

Karl went inside; he came close to me with tears in his eyes. He could not talk, but he only planted a kiss on my forehead because there were pipes connected to my mouth.

He held my hand softly.

"Oma dear, I remembered when I was in the hospital just like you, your talk made me fight. I was stabbed because of you, and now you were hit by a car because of me. Oma, I know you don't give up. I know you can hear me. Please, my angel, don't give up. You must fight with all your strength. You have to fight to survive." He said, still crying.

"Mama is outside killing herself with tears because of you; Terry and Jamila are also outside waiting for you to wake up. Oma, please fight this," he added.

I was suspended in a state of semi-consciousness, unsure of what was real and what was just a dream. But then, Karl's voice pierced through the haze, his words imbuing me with a sense of clarity. He extended his hand, and I felt an overwhelming urge to take it, as if it was a lifeline pulling me back to reality. As I opened my eyes, the world around me snapped into focus, and Karl's face was the first thing I saw. His eyes shone with relief and joy, and he leaned in closer, his lips brushing against mine in a soft, gentle kiss.

"Oma, you're awake. Thank God. I love you," he whispered, his voice trembling with emotion as he scattered kisses across my forehead.

The tenderness of the moment was almost overwhelming, and I felt my heart swell with love and gratitude for this man who had been by my side through thick and thin.

I had no strength to talk; I was just staring at him. He called Mama, Terry, and Jamila to come inside, but the nurse did not allow them inside, so I had to be left alone.

CHAPTER ELEVEN

When the nurse asked them to leave, I closed my eyes again. Throughout the night, I did not open my eyes. Karl was outside all through the night; he did not go home. Terry and Jamila took Mama home. Jamila made her food, but she refused to eat. When my Mum called me the next day, Mama told her I was at the hospital, but I was getting better. Mama also explained the whole ordeal to her. My Mum started crying and lamenting. Mama convinced her that I would be alright, promising her that I would be back in Nigeria once I recovered.

"All you need to do now is to pray for her recovery," Mama said.

I spent three days in a state of unresponsiveness, unable to open my eyes or move. The doctors informed Karl that I had slipped into a coma due to excessive blood loss. For three days, I remained unconscious, leaving Karl in a state of distress. He devoted himself to praying for my recovery, barely taking time to eat or sleep. His days were spent by my side, with occasional visits to the chapel for solace. Mama was equally affected, refusing to eat as she worried about my well-being. Terry and Jamila also came very often to see Oma at the hospital. They begged Mama to eat, but she refused. Mama kept praying and coming to the hospital. I never knew Mama loved me so much; maybe it's because I've been staying with her for over three years.

A week after the accident, I regained consciousness; Karl was the first person I saw when I opened my eyes.

"Oma, you are awake," Karl said as he saw my eyes open.

He came closer and kissed me. He went to call the doctor. The doctor came in with two nurses. The doctor was a nice man.

"Welcome back, my dear," the doctor said while smiling at me.

With gentle care, the doctor carefully removed the nasal oxygen tube that had been providing me with a steady flow of oxygen. Next, he turned his attention to monitoring my vital signs, beginning with a check of my body temperature, a crucial indicator of my overall health and well-being.

The doctor looked at me and said, "You are a strong lady; the Lord has a purpose for bringing you back to life; many people that had the same case with you don't last for two days before they died. But here you are, after one week, you still regain consciousness."

I smiled at him, and he left.

Karl quickly called Terry and Mama to share the joyful news. Soon after, they arrived at the hospital, eager to see me. Mama's face lit up with happiness when she laid eyes on me. She couldn't contain her excitement, beaming with joy as she danced around the room.

"Feifei!" she exclaimed, using her affectionate nickname for me.

She rushed to my side, her eyes brimming with tears, and gently kissed my forehead. Terry and Jamila followed suit, each planting a tender kiss on my forehead as they basked in the joy of my recovery.

"At least Mama can now eat," Jamila said.

Mama turned and said to her, "Now that my Feifei is back, I will eat as much food as you want me to eat." We all laughed at her.

Karl kissed me every single time. And anytime he kissed me, Mama, Terry, and Jamila would laugh because he was acting funny.

"Karl," Terry called. "If I were you, once Oma recovers, I won't waste a minute asking her to marry me; I would wed her immediately." We all burst into laughter.

Karl turned to me and was staring at me. He gave me a lasting kiss on the lips; his lips were still on mine when Mama beat him at his back.

"Do you want to kill her with kisses? Can't you see she had not fully recovered?" We all laughed again, and he removed his lips.

Just then, a nurse came in; she wanted to inject me, and she asked everyone to leave because it would make me sleep. So they all left. Karl rushed to his house to freshen up and buy me fruits and food. Mama ate a lot of food. And then she left with Terry and Jamila.

After three hours of sleep, I woke up and saw Karl beside me on the bed. He brought out the fruits he had bought and fed me. He also brought a love-shaped balloon with the inscription, "*Get well soon, my darling princess.*" After feeding me, he handed the balloon to me. I smiled and thanked him.

Karl stayed by my side that night, and the following morning, he informed the doctor that someone was after my life. The doctor then assigned him two securities. I was surprised when he told me about it.

"Is this the hospital where your cousin works?" I asked him.

"Yes," he replied.

"Do you think someone was actually after my life?" I asked.

"Oma, please don't start this again. All these happened because of your stubbornness. Assuming you allowed me to drive you home or even follow you, I believe you won't be here now," he said angrily.

But he apologized immediately for sounding harsh at me.

"I don't like being angry at you. I just want you to recover on time. I missed you so much," Karl said.

"I am sorry for all that happened, too," I said.

He kissed me, "I've forgiven you. I love you, Oma, and I won't want anything bad to happen to you. If I lose you, then my children's mother will be gone, and I don't think I can marry any other woman except you, my love." He said, smiling lovingly at me. I slept off, and he left to freshen up.

The security men were standing in front of the door when a nurse came into my room. She injected the drip I was receiving.

"Let me see how you will survive this time around. Goodbye, Oma," the nurse said when trying to inject the last medicine into my drip.

"Sasha! What are you doing here? And why are you dressed like a nurse? And what are you injecting in her drip?" Karl entered, shouting profusely.

Immediately, Sasha injected the medicine into my drip and increased its speed.

Karl rushed in and slapped her, making her fall hard. The security guards heard the slap and rushed in. I started feeling weird, like something was happening inside me. I curled up, shivering like crazy, my teeth chattering, and my breathing getting shorter. I think the drug Sasha put in my IV was kicking in. Karl rang the emergency bell, and immediately, many doctors and nurses came into the ward. They ordered everyone to leave the room.

Sasha was tied, and the police came, handcuffed her and took her away. Before the police took her away, she turned and looked at Karl.

"Since I can't have you, then no other woman will ever have you," Sasha said, smiling devilishly.

"Oma will be dead in the next thirty minutes," she added. One of the police officers slapped her and pulled her away.

Karl called Mama and Terry and told them what had happened; they came immediately. The doctors were injecting me while the nurses removed the drip Sasha injected. One of the doctors went to get something, and Karl rushed to him and asked him if I was OK.

"The poison the lady injected was very deadly, and it might kill her if her system is not strong because she just had an accident."

The doctor hastily left after saying, "I'm afraid to tell you that her chances of survival are very slim because some of her body systems were affected and have become weak.

Mama screamed as she heard what the doctor said.

"Oh no! My Feifei can't die," she cried out, rolling on the floor.

Terry was consoling her, but Karl went close to the door and was watching me. Mama and Terry came there too. They were all praying in their hearts for me to survive. Mama kept remembering all that we used to do, the way I laughed, the present I gave her on her birthday, and other lovely moments we shared together. Terry also reflected on the moments we spent together. His eyes were welling with tears.

"God, please don't let Oma die; please give her the strength to fight and survive." He whispered silently to himself.

Karl was crying like a baby. Lovely days kept flashing back at him. He kept remembering the way I smiled when we first met and the days when we actually played.

"God, please help the mother of my kids to survive. I promise to serve you always. Please don't let Oma die; You saved her once; You will do it again, please, Lord, I beg of You," he prayed silently.

I continued to shake until the doctor gave me an injection, and then, I stopped.

"Her heartbeat is beating slowly, the EKG tracing is reading low, and the waves are going down," a nurse shouted.

The news frightened the medical team, and one of the female doctors explained what was happening.

"She's having a cardiac arrest, and each second of non-profusion means tissue loss!"

She then demanded a paddle electrode defibrillator, which was given to her immediately as the nurses monitored the wave of the machine. On hearing the word "clear," the doctor placed the electrode paddle on my chest, and I sprung up in shock. This process was repeated three times, but all efforts to revive me proved abortive as the life support machine showed a straight line, which meant I was dead.

Karl, standing outside and watching through the glass of the door, broke down in tears as he saw my lifeless body on the bed. It was 2:30 p.m. when I gave up the ghost, and I can't describe the pain Mama and my beloved friends went through.

On hearing the news, Mama fainted immediately, and Terry was shouting for help as they tried to revive her. Karl broke into the room where my body lay and started calling out my name loudly while crying.

Suddenly, they all heard a beeping noise from the life support machine, and some wavelengths started appearing. Karl, with tears in his eyes, couldn't contain his joy as he kissed me passionately.

Immediately, Mama heard I was back to life; she stood up and began thanking God while the doctors and everyone else were so amazed because my resurrection was a great miracle. They were all asked to stay outside as the doctors tried running some checks on me to know if I was truly alright. I escaped death again, and I was happy that I wouldn't have to leave my loved ones with grief in their heart.

After checking my pulse, the female doctor gave me an injection. The medical staff left the room after another drip was placed, and the doctor instructed them to give me more time to recover before they came to check on me again. It was like a dream when my heart stopped beating. I would have died if not for a beautiful woman who appeared before me. She told me to go back and that it was not yet time for me to come. Her beauty is unlike anything I have ever seen. The woman told me she was the Blessed Virgin Mary. I thanked her and went back. That was when tears began to flow from my eyes. I slept throughout the day, and it was only the next day that I opened my eyes.

Karl was very happy when the nurse called to tell him that I was awake. When he saw the tears in my eyes, he came and cleaned it and planted a kiss on my left cheek.

"Don't cry, dear; thank God you are awake. I will never ever leave you again. I'm so sorry I left that day." he said and smiled.

Mama and Terry came in, too. Mama held me tight, whispering some words as tears rolled down her eyes. I guess she must be thanking God.

My colleagues at work came and visited me at the hospital with presents. Two of my closest friends came and sang and danced to my favourite Chinese song. I laughed so hard. Some of my classmates came with Terry, too, and they brought their presents, too. Mama's relatives came the next day. I was so happy to be surrounded by people who sincerely loved me.

When I recovered a little and was able to talk well, I asked Karl to call my parents, and he did. So we spoke with them. As usual, my Mum kept pestering me to come back to Nigeria." Oma, please come back to Nigeria. I just want to see you, my dear. Please come back," she said.

I promised her that I would come back once I was fully recovered.

Karl told them how Sasha wanted to kill me, and we had other discussions, too, and ended the call.

"Oma dear, once you recover, we are travelling back to Nigeria with or without a transfer letter," Karl said, and I nodded my head in agreement.

Two weeks later, my boss came to the hospital with flowers and a card to wish me well. He heard about the incident and came to give me an envelope.

"This is your transfer letter; you will be working with our branch in Nigeria," he said. I was very happy, and I thanked him.

"The only thing is that I and other workers will miss you," he said

"I will also miss you all," I replied, smiling. Karl also thanked him, and he left.

"Sweetheart, we will be leaving for Nigeria once you fully recover. Now we have your transfer letter, and I'm done with my work here. So please try to recover fully so you will be discharged, so that we can travel back to our fatherland. Karl said

"What about Sasha? Where is she?" I asked.

"She is in police custody. She will be taken to court, and her final hearing will be next week," he replied.

"But why do you think she hates me to the extent of trying to kill me by all means?" I asked.

He sighed deeply.

"According to what she said, you snatched me away from her, and if she doesn't have me, no woman will."

He shook his head mournfully.

"She was ready to do anything to have me. Unfortunately for her, she didn't know you survived; she would be thinking that you are dead."

CHAPTER TWELVE

The day of Sasha's final court appearance had finally dawned, bringing with it a sense of closure and reckoning. As she stood in the dock, her eyes fixed on the presiding judge, the air was thick with anticipation.

The judge, his expression solemn and unyielding, began to deliver his verdict:

"Sasha Richard, after careful consideration of the evidence presented before this court, I find you guilty on all counts. Your actions have been deemed a serious affront to the law, and accordingly, you will face the consequences. I hereby sentence you to fifteen years of imprisonment, to be served with hard labour. This sentence will be followed by your deportation to your country of origin, where you will be expected to abide by the laws and regulations of that land."

The judge's words, firm and unyielding, brought an end to the proceedings, sealing Sasha's fate and marking the beginning of a new chapter in her life. Sasha was handcuffed and taken away. On her way to the van, Karl went to her, moved closer, and whispered,

"Sorry, my dear Sasha. I hope you enjoy the choice you made. Goodbye, my former lover." He laughed and walked away.

Sasha was put at the back of the van and driven to the prison.

When Karl came back to the hospital, he told me how everything had gone. I was not happy because Sasha was imprisoned; I felt bad for her. I have heard stories about prison life, and all those stories were nothing to write home about. I really pitied her.

"But I am happy that you are safe now, and I won't have to worry about that evil woman," Karl said and hugged me.

As I continued to recover, I was touched by the steady stream of visitors who came to check on me, making me feel loved and cherished. Karl would often surprise me by arranging for two of my colleagues to visit and perform my favorite songs, complete with dancing, whenever I was experiencing discomfort. His thoughtful gestures helped alleviate my pain and lifted my spirits. Karl's devotion was unwavering; he remained by my side constantly, only taking brief breaks to freshen up before returning to my bedside. His tireless efforts to pamper and care for me made a significant difference in my recovery, reducing my pain and filling my heart with gratitude.

My parents kept calling to see how I was doing and to remind me about my return to Nigeria. My Mum sometimes teased me about getting married, but I always ended up changing the topic.

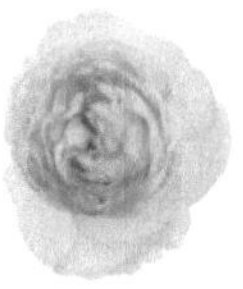

Two months later, I was discharged from the hospital; I could walk well and do things on my own, but I was instructed not to do anything stressful. Karl and Mama have always been amazing. They wouldn't let me do anything, pampering me like a newborn child. The only things I was allowed to do were eat, bathe, and sleep. Karl started making preparations for our journey back to Nigeria.

"Everything will be ready in two weeks, so don't stop preparing to go home," Karl said, relaxing on the couch.

"Are you arranging for Mama too? Because I would want her to follow us to Nigeria, to spend at least two weeks with us," I asked.

"But we have to ask her about that," he replied.

I nodded my head in agreement.

But when I told Mama about our plans and intentions to take her with us, she declined. She said she preferred to be in China than go to any other country. This made me sad.

A week after I was discharged, I went back to the hospital for my final checkup. I was told that I was completely fine, but I should not stress myself for three months. I thanked the doctors and left. When my Mum called, I was happy to announce our journey back to Nigeria to her. My mother was the happiest person after I told her of my plans to return home.

"I can't wait to see you." My mother said over the phone.

"Brother Chimaobi was angry at me for not attending his traditional wedding; he would be furious if I didn't attend his white wedding." I said to her.

I told Mum about Mama's objection to her coming with us to Nigeria.

Karl announced to me that a send-forth party would be coming up on Thursday so that I would say goodbye to my friends. Thursday came, and the party began. I was called to give a speech. I collected the microphone, feeling so nervous.

"I appreciate the presence of everyone here, and also those who are unable to come due to some reasons," I said.

"My biggest thanks goes to God Almighty, who gave me life. I also want to sincerely thank my love, Karl, who has been there for me throughout my stay at the hospital."

Karl smiled.

"Mama, thank you so much for your care since I arrived in China. I just can't repay you enough. You're indeed my second mother." Mama came to where I was and hugged me.

"I also appreciate Terry and his lover, Jamila. They are the best friends I have here in China. Thanks so much. My appreciation also goes to Mama's relatives, friends, and well-wishers who cared for and prayed for me when I was hospitalized. Thanks to you all."

"You are welcome," they all chorused in the Chinese dialect.

I smiled and continued.

"Finally, I want to thank my boss and colleagues at Bright Hope company. Titi and Shun, I appreciate you guys. Thanks a lot for your dance while I was in the hospital."

They stood, sang, and danced. Everyone in the auditorium was amazed at their funny dancing steps, and they all clapped.

"Thanks to everyone I mentioned and those I forgot to mention. I say a big thank you to you all. May the good Lord bless you. I love you all," I said, dropping the microphone and leaving the podium.

Everyone stood up and clapped for me.

Terry went to the podium and picked up the microphone.

"I have an announcement to make," he said.

We were all eager to know what the announcement is all about. The atmosphere in the room was electric as Terry suddenly departed from the podium, his movements fluid and deliberate as he made his way to Jamila. Dropping to one knee, he revealed a small, exquisite box containing a ring, its sparkle catching the light. His eyes locked onto Jamila's, shining with sincerity and adoration, as he asked the question that would change their lives forever:

"Jamila, will you marry me?" The room was transfixed, with all of us holding our collective breath in anticipation of her response.

Jamila's face illuminated with a radiant smile as she responded, her voice filled with emotion,

"Yes, I will!" Terry's eyes shone with tears of joy as he slid the ring onto her finger, sealing their commitment.

As they shared a tender, passionate kiss, the room exploded into applause, with cheers and congratulations pouring forth from the assembled crowd.

"Oma and Karl, I hope you will be present at our wedding. We also invite everyone here to grace the occasion," Terry said.

"Wow! That's wonderful. We will surely be present at your wedding," I said.

CHAPTER THIRTEEN

We rescheduled our flight to Monday to attend Terry and Jamila's wedding, which was a beautiful and intimate celebration. I was honoured to serve as Jamila's maid of honour, while Karl stood by Terry's side as his best man. Despite the tight timeline, the wedding was meticulously planned and executed, filled with love, laughter, and joy. Terry later revealed to me that he had been secretly planning the wedding for some time, intent on surprising Jamila with the perfect day.

The day after the wedding, Karl, Mama, and I went to visit Terry and Jamila. We had fun for the whole day, and then, at sunset, we left for our respective houses. Everything was already in place. The next day, Terry, Jamila, Mama, and some of her relatives, as well as Titi and Shun, escorted us to the airport. When it was time to board the plane, Karl and I hugged them all.

Tears welled in my eyes when I moved to Mama for a hug.

“Stop crying, my baby girl. You should pay me some visit from time to time,” Mama said while cleaning my tears with her index fingers.

“Make sure you guys get married and have kids. I would like to see your children so I can tell them the love story of their father and mother,” She added.

We laughed, and I hurriedly hugged her and left so that we wouldn’t miss our flight. Twenty minutes later, we took off. As I gazed out the window, my eyes welled up with tears, already feeling the pangs of separation from our loved ones. Karl, sensing my distress, brought out a handkerchief and gently dabbed away my tears. He wrapped his arms around me, and I nestled my head against his chest, finding comfort in his warmth and closeness.

“This was the same way I was shedding tears when I was coming to China; I was crying because I thought I wouldn’t see you again. I didn’t know what fate had for me in China; now, I am crying because I am already missing those I love.” I said.

“That’s life, but you can always come and visit, just like Mama said,” Karl said, patting my shoulder.

Before I knew what was happening, Karl was sleeping. I gently raised my head from his shoulder and kept staring at him as he slept peacefully. Then I discovered that the lady opposite us had been looking at Karl. Maybe she was admiring him—who knows? I kissed Karl on the lips to let her know that he was a no-go area for her. She turned and continued reading the novel in her hands. I laughed, leaned back on his shoulder, and slept off.

We woke up when the plane was ready to land. We boarded the second plane that would take us to Nigeria. When we arrived at Nnamdi Azikiwe airport, a car was already waiting for us. We both entered the car, and the driver zoomed off. I observed that the car wasn't going in the direction of my parent's house, and I became anxious.

"Karl, where are we going? This doesn't look like the road to my father's house," I said

"Don't worry, dear," he said as he concentrated on his phone.

"But I want to see my parents first before anything else," I said.

"You will surely see them; just calm down," he replied, planting a kiss on my right cheek.

As the car proceeded, it eventually came to a halt in front of a majestic mansion that resembled a castle, complete with a grand, imposing gate. The gate swung open, and the car glided through the entrance.

"Wow!" I exclaimed in awe of the breathtaking sight before me. The sheer beauty of the house, with its meticulously manicured surroundings, left me stunned. Feeling a mix of excitement and nervousness, I turned to Karl.

"Where are we?" I asked, my voice tinged with curiosity and a hint of trepidation.

"I know this isn't your parents' house, but just relax. Everything will be alright. You will surely see your parents," he replied.

"I just reserved some surprises for you," he added.

"Don't tell me you brought me to the famous diamond castle?" I asked Karl, who had been smiling at my reactions.

He came down and opened the door for me. I came down gently. I saw a man and woman whom I thought should be in their early 60s. They looked familiar and I remembered that I had seen them at the hospital when Karl was stabbed. Also, there was a lady and a young man standing beside them at the entrance door. Karl went and hugged them all. "Oma, this man here is my father, this is my mother, and these are my siblings," he said as he pointed to them one after the other.

I was so surprised because I never saw this coming.

I immediately bowed before the man, and he patted my back. I did the same to the woman, but she hugged me instead.

"You are welcome, dear," Karl's Mum said sweetly.

The lady came and hugged me, too.

"I am Tessy Udechukwu," said the lady.

Likewise, the young man also hugged me.

"My name is Desmond Udechukwu," the young man said.

"I am Omasirichi Percy. It's nice meeting you all," I said while smiling.

After the introduction, the door opened, and both my parents and siblings came out. I was surprised because that was the least I was expecting; my Mum and Dad were smiling at me. I ran to them and hugged them all; Simdi and her husband and children were there, too, and Chimaobi and his wife were also there.

"Hope you love the surprise?" Karl asked jokingly

"Yes, I love it so much. But why did you choose to do it in a hotel and not at my house or yours?" I asked innocently, and everyone burst into laughter, including Karl.

I was shocked because I wasn't expecting anyone to laugh at what I said.

Karl moved closer to me and whispered into my ears, "This is my father's house and not a hotel."

I opened my mouth wide in shock. "Is Karl's parents rich?" I asked myself. I never knew Karl was from a very wealthy background. He is really humble.

"You have a beautiful mansion, sir," I said to Mr. Udechukwu, who was smiling at me.

Mr. Udechukwu invited us all into his mansion. They had all prepared a celebration party for our return. I saw all my relatives at the party; it was indeed a surprise to me. There was a lot to eat and drink. The rhythm of the music was what I desired. Karl moved closer to me, "Can I have a dance with my angel?" he asked.

I gave in to his request. Suddenly, the music stopped, and right in front of me, Karl went on his knees. He brought a small red box and opened it. The centre of the box held a stunning diamond ring that was carefully placed there. I was astounded.

"I've always wanted to spend the rest of my life with you. Today will surely bring my wish to reality. Will you marry me, Omasirichi Percy?" Karl said softly.

None of these were what I had anticipated; today was just full of surprises. I couldn't move my lips; I just kept on staring at him. Everyone was expecting me to say something fantastic. I got hold of myself.

I turned away from Karl to pick up the microphone. Karl was confused; everyone was also confused.

"Karl Udechukwu, I, Omasirichi Percy, will marry you," I said slowly with tears in my eyes.

Everyone shouted in excitement; they must have been anxious to know my response. Karl stood up, held my hand and placed the diamond ring on my finger. He kissed me passionately. Everyone kept clapping and shouting.

"What a romantic and dramatic way to say yes," Karl whispered to my ears, and we both laughed.

Karl's mother came close to me, hugged me, and whispered, " Welcome to the Udechukwu family."

"Thank you, ma," I said.

My Mum came and hugged me too.

People started congratulating us. Mr. Udechukwu took the microphone to talk, "Let the engagement party phase begin," he shouted in excitement.

The DJ played songs, and we continued dancing.

After the party, I followed my parents to our house. When we got home, I asked my Mum, "How did all this happen?"

"Karl sent his parents to our house to make the whole arrangement; more surprises are yet to come, my dear," she replied.

"Oh, Mum, I'm overwhelmed with surprises already. Please tell me what other surprises await me." I said in a childlike manner.

My Mum smiled at me. "It will surprise you to know that your wedding has already been planned. When Karl told you he travelled to Hong Kong, it wasn't for a business trip; he went there to buy some of the things you would need for the wedding. And your wedding is in three weeks; here are your invitation cards," she said as she brought out the cards and showed them to me.

"It is indeed a surprise. Karl was very sure I would marry him. Well, I'm happy about it, and I want to say thank you to you, Mum, Dad, ChiSimdi and Chimaobi," I said.

"Chimaobi's wedding is this Saturday. Luckily, you came beforehand; otherwise, your brother would have been mad at you," my Mum said, and we both laughed.

I was chosen as the maid of honour for Chimaobi's wife to be. I actually wanted to object since I believe she should have a friend to do that for her. However, I learned that she willingly chose me, and I saw it as a great privilege, so I accepted the proposal.

As I entered my room, I was enveloped in a sense of familiarity and comfort. The space was just as I had left it, with every item in its designated place, creating a sense of continuity and normalcy. After indulging in a relaxing bath, my mother's gentle voice summoned me to join them for dinner, but I politely declined, still feeling pleasantly full from the party earlier in the day. The combination of being back home, surrounded by the warmth and love of my family, and the happiness of the party, had left me feeling content and at peace. I settled into bed, feeling the softness of the blankets and the gentle give of the mattress, and let my gaze drift to the beautiful ring on my finger. The sparkle of the diamond and the elegance of the design seemed to shine even brighter in the quiet of my room, serving as a poignant reminder of the special day. With a sense of gratitude and joy, I picked up the phone and dialled Mama's number, eager to share the wonderful news with her.

I told her that I would like her to be present on my wedding day, and she responded positively. She wished me well and congratulated me. I ended the call, adjusted myself properly in bed, and slept off.

The next day, Karl's call woke me up. We had lovely discussions for over two hours. After that, I went downstairs and prayed with the rest of the family members. I made breakfast, and we all ate happily. Shortly after our meal was over, ChiSimdi and her kids arrived. She said her children had been asking about me, so she decided to bring them to see me.

"Good morning, Aunty," Angel and Percy Junior greeted me, and I hugged them.

"Percy looks just like dad," I said.

"That was the reason we named him Percy Junior," Simdi replied

"You must have a lot of gist for me, and I also have a lot of it too," Simdi said as we both ran to my room.

We chatted till lunchtime passed, and Mum did not bother calling us to eat.

Karl came, we had a brief discussion, and he left. I went back to my room to meet Simdi and continued chatting with her. In the midst of our discussion, I remembered that I hadn't called Terry and Jamila to inform them about the good news. I called them immediately and told them about my wedding. They were so happy for me. My sister and I continued chatting till night, and we slept off.

The next morning, we went to Chimaobi's place to see how far they had gone with the preparations and helped him with some other things. Two days later, we went to church to celebrate with Chimaobi and his wife, Edna. I was wearing a long gown that was simple but wonderful. The gown looked so good on me that people stared at me instead of the bride. Edna chose the gown for me herself.

"I'm proud of your beauty, darling," Karl whispered to my ear. I smiled at him.

After the Mass and photo section, we went to the reception hall. After entertaining and exchanging gifts, the wedding came to an end, and Chimaobi was the happiest man on earth that day. Edna is a beautiful, tall, and well-mannered girl. I once told her that their children would surely be handsome and beautiful because Chimaobi, my brother, is a handsome man, and she is a beautiful woman. After the wedding, Karl dropped me at my place. He came down to kiss me, but I pushed him away from me playfully.

"You will not kiss or touch me till after our wedding," I said, smiling and moving towards the door. I entered the house, winked at him and closed the door.

He smiled at me and whispered, "You will be mine soonest," and he left.

CHAPTER FOURTEEN

Some time back, Karl had asked me to accompany him on a trip to Hong Kong. Now, just a week before our wedding, he showed up at my place, carrying a large box. He handed it to me and asked me to open it. As I lifted the lid, I was amazed to find a stunning wedding gown inside. But what caught my attention was that the gown seemed eerily familiar.

"Oh yes, it does look familiar. Do you remember the wedding gown you saw and loved at the mall when we went to Hong Kong? So this is it," Karl said, smiling at me.

"Karl, you will never cease to amaze me. You bought it for me? You are such a darling," I said while hugging him passionately.

As I was about to kiss him, he shifted back.

"No kissing until our wedding night; remember the deal, baby," he said and laughed. I was a bit embarrassed. "Mr. Handsome, do you think you're that attractive for me to kiss you?" I said, trying to cover up.

"I know I am that sexy, and you can't wait to taste these lips, and my dear Miss Beauty, these lips here won't kiss you until our wedding night," he replied while touching his lips.

I hit him on the back and ran inside. He pursued me and caught me. I looked at him romantically. "You're such a blessing to me, Karl. God bless the day I met you," I said.

He kissed my chin, and when he wanted to kiss me on the lips, I stood up and wanted to run past him, but he pulled me back. "But this man can no longer wait till the wedding night," Karl said and kissed me.

Just then, my sister came in and coughed to attract our attention. She greeted Karl and threw a newspaper at me.

"You are all over the news," she shouted.

I picked up the newspaper on the floor and checked the headline: "Chief Udechukwu's son is engaged and will be married next Saturday to Miss Omasirichi Percy."

I was surprised, and I turned to Karl. "You never told me you are a wealthy celebrity," I said. He laughed.

I read down the page, and I saw things that surprised me the most. "So you came to China to open a new branch of your father's company, yet you told me you are just a worker there. Now I understand why you were not bothered about going to work during those times Sasha was threatening me," I said.

"So what other surprises will you spring up on me?" I asked

"Now you know more about my background. And for the rest of the surprises, just watch as I unfold things," Karl said.

My sister and I sighed. I showed her my beautiful wedding gown, and she was so excited.

"You will definitely look like a princess on your wedding day. But where did you buy the gown?" She asked.

Karl explained how he got it from Hong Kong without letting me know about it. ChiSimdi turned to Karl, "You are truly the best man for my sister, and she is lucky to have you. I pray your love for her grows and never fades," she said to him.

"I am flattered," he said.

"I'm not flattering you dear; I'm just saying the truth," Simdi said. Karl thanked her, and we all smiled.

My sister collected the newspaper and left. Karl pushed me closer to himself and tickled me. I pushed him away and ran; he pursued me till we got outside. While I was running outside, I saw my Mum, and I ran to her.

"Mum, please save me from Karl. He wants to catch me," I said, acting like a child.

Karl came closer to my Mum, but she stopped him from touching me. "Mr. Karl, it is not yet time for you to take my daughter, so please leave her alone," My Mum said jokingly.

"Mum, I've paid her dowry as tradition demands, so she is already my wife. Please, let her go," Karl said.

My Mum shifted, Karl caught me, and we all started laughing. His phone rang, and he had a little discussion on the phone. After answering the call, he kissed me on my forehead and left.

"He is just funny; he won't stop making me laugh. I pray you guys continue to love each other," My Mum said.

We went inside, and I showed her my wedding gown and the newspaper. She was very happy.

"Your aunts and cousins will be arriving tomorrow to lend a hand with the preparations," she said with a smile.

"I'm sure you're getting everything ready, because your wedding is going to be the most talked-about event in town!" We both laughed.

The countdown had begun - just 48 hours until the wedding, and the house was a whirlwind of activity, with everyone working tirelessly to ensure a perfect celebration. Karl ensured everything was going well. I didn't have to bother about my maid of honour.

"I will be calm and watch everything unfold," I told him before he said it to me.

The next day was bachelor's night and my bridal shower. Those who went to the bachelor's night said it was fabulous, and my bridal shower was also fantastic. I was already getting tired. Karl advised me to rest on time so I won't look tired for the big event tomorrow. The day had finally come—it was my moment. I woke up brimming with excitement. Even though I got up late, no one had bothered to wake me up on time. I came downstairs; I saw my Mum moving closer to me. "Why haven't you had your bathe? The makeup artist Karl called is here. I will bring you your breakfast once it's ready." My Mum shouted. I went back to my room to bathe. My Mum brought my breakfast, and she made sure I ate before she left my room. The makeup artist started his work. He is just so good at his work.

When it was exactly ten o'clock, a white limousine car stopped in front of our house, and my picture was on it. My cousin came and told me that the car was waiting for me. After the makeup was done, I wore my wedding gown.

"You look super beautiful!" Simdi shouted in excitement.

She held my hand, and we went downstairs. There were three men in uniform; they looked like security men from the castle. As they saw me coming, one of them opened the door of the white limousine for me to enter. I entered, and they closed the door for me. My parents and sister joined the black limousine at the back with two other security men.

They drove us to the church, and the security men came and opened the door for me. I saw pressmen and journalists moving closer to me, flashing cameras at me. But with the help of the security men, I was able to walk through the walkway without disturbance from the press.

I saw Titi and Shun moving behind me while holding my long gown. I was surprised to see them, and they told me they were part of my bridal train. They were dressed in the same design, and they looked beautiful. I was walking towards the door, and my Dad, Mum, and sister came down from the car and were waiting for me at the door.

As I approached the church, my Dad held my hand. He walked me down the aisle while everyone stood up. I began to remember the first day I met Karl, how we started, the troubles we overcame together, when he was rushed to the hospital and how I cried. Here I was, walking down the aisle to marry the man I love.

"Thank you, Lord, for making all my dreams become a reality," I said to myself.

The same thoughts were going through Karl's mind.

"I thought I had lost her, but my dreams are becoming a reality. I am getting married to the woman I love. Thank You, Lord, for this is the day you have made," he whispered to himself.

My Dad took me to the altar and handed me over to Karl.

"Here is my daughter. Please take very good care of her. She is my diamond," he said, and Karl took my hand. We knelt before the priest, who blessed our union. After the necessary prayers, it was time to exchange rings. The ring bearer brought the rings, and we took our vows. Karl asked the priest to permit him to make the vow himself.

Karl took the ring and looked at me, holding my hand so passionately.

"Oma, when I thought I lost you, I never knew what else to do or what direction to take. But when you recovered, I found out that I didn't want to live without you in my life. We have gone through many trials and challenges, and we overcame them all. Right now, I am standing before everyone present and most especially, I stand before God Almighty to say that I, Karl Udechukwu, promise to love you eternally, in good health and in bad times. I make you, Miss Omasirichi Percy, my wife in the name of the Father and of the Son and of the Holy Spirit."

The whole congregation chorused "Amen" and clapped.

He inserted the ring on my finger.

I also took the ring and looked directly into Karl's eyes.

"Karl Udechukwu, you are my first love. You've been my strength since I set my eyes on you. Your words have kept me going. I declare in front of everyone present and in front of the Most High God, who has blessed our union from the first day we met. I promise to love you eternally, in sickness and in health, in sorrow and in joy, until death do us part. And this day, in front of everybody and in front of God Almighty, I, Omasirichi Percy, make you my husband in the name of the Father and of the Son and the Holy Spirit."

I inserted the ring on his finger, and the congregation chorused, "Amen!".

They all clapped.

The priest declared, "I hereby pronounced them as Husband and wife. You may kiss the bride."

Karl came closer to me, opened my veil, and gave me a passionate kiss. His kiss tasted different, maybe because today was a special day in our lives. The congregation kept on clapping, and the cameras were rolling on.

"You are the most beautiful woman I have ever seen, and I have a surprise for you," Karl whispered to my ear.

"What surprise?" I asked.

He pointed in one direction in the church. My eyes followed his hand, and I saw Mama, Terry, and Jamila.

"Oh Karl, you are the best husband in the world," I said and kissed him again, and people started clapping again.

We exchanged pleasantries with everyone, especially Mama, Terry, and Jamila. I was so happy to see them.

After the church service, we took several pictures. The pressmen were all over us. After the picture section, we entered the limousine, which now had a picture of Karl and I on it, and we drove to the reception hall.

It was a very beautiful place with a lovely house that was designed. A ribbon was tied at the entrance of the house. When we got there, people were already waiting for us; even our parents were there.

"This is the second to the last surprise I have for you today, sweetheart; let's go and open our new house," he said and smiled.

I was amazed that I opened my mouth wide. Karl held my hand, and we moved towards the entrance. The priest prayed and blessed it, Karl gave me a scissors, and I cut the ribbon. Everybody started clapping, and we all went inside. The interior decoration was just the same as the hotel we lodged in when we went for tourism in China. It was just like the diamond castle in Barbie movies.

"Do you like the house?" Karl asked

"I don't just like it; I love it," I shouted in excitement.

After going around the house, we went outside and continued with the wedding reception. Everyone ate to their satisfaction, gifts were exchanged, and we celebrated. I received a gorgeous gold necklace as a gift from Mama. I thanked her and hugged her.

"I never knew Karl was from a rich family," Mama said.

"I didn't know either. He has been loading me with surprises," I replied.

"My dear Feifei, I am happy for you," Mama said as she hugged me again. The party continued until 6 p.m.

when people started leaving. By 8 p.m., Karl's family entered the black limousine and left for their house.

Mama, Terry, and Jamila followed my parents to their house because they would be spending some days with us before going back to China. Terry and Jamila will only stay for a week before they travel back to China, likewise Titi and Shun. After they left, Karl went upstairs, and after some time, he came downstairs to continue with the merriment.

CHAPTER FIFTEEN

Around 10 p.m., everybody had gone to their respective homes. The servants were left to clean the environment. We waited until they were done cleaning, and then they left. Karl took me inside and locked the door.

"Prepare for the last surprise of the day," he said.

He blindfolded me and led me to the room. He instructed me to take off my blinds, which I did. As I entered the room, I marvelled at what I saw. I was struck by its grandeur and elegant decor. A majestic bed, adorned with a crisp white bed sheet, dominated the space. Delicate petals were intricately arranged in a heart shape on the bed, exuding romance and warmth. My gaze wandered to the wall, where a beautifully framed picture of Karl and me hung prominently. The room was bathed in a soft, warm glow, courtesy of the colourful candles and a subtle red light that added a touch of intimacy to the ambiance. Soft, melancholic love music filled the air, setting a romantic yet introspective mood. A sleek, red dress, its skimpy design hinting at a sensual evening, lay draped across the cushion. On the nearby table, a chilled bottle of champagne stood ready, accompanied by two delicate glasses, poised to toast a special moment.

Karl walked up to me, with a big smile on his face he said, "Go to the bathroom now, have a cool bath, and wear this," pointing to the dress on the cushion.

I went straight to the bathroom. After bathing, I cleaned myself and wore the red skimpy dress. Karl just kept on staring at me.

"You look so sexy right now," he said as he walked up to me with a glass of wine.

I collected it and sat on the bed, sipping my wine. He held my hand for a dance. I stood up to dance with him.

"You look very beautiful, Oma. I am happy you are now my wife," he said softly.

"I am happy you are now my husband," I replied.

In a flash, Karl carried me to the bed. He kissed me on my neck, down to my chest. He moved back to kiss my lips. I could feel the passion, which made me moan with pleasure. My body began to respond to his lovemaking, and pressing my body against him, returning his kisses. My head was reeling as his kisses became more urgent and tender. I flung my arms around his neck, and then fingers stroked his back. His hand caressed my most secret spot; I knew nothing but the desire to belong to him completely; the pain, as he took my body for his own, was momentary. I was soaring to unknown heights of rapture with him, our bodies as one body, as with shuddering sighs of delight. We whispered each other's name in pleasure. We lay still in each other's arms and slept off.

When I woke up, the sky was beginning to lighten. For a moment, I wondered why I felt so happy and content, and then, the events of the night flashed through my mind. For a moment, I felt I must have dreamt it, but then, I became aware of Karl's warm body beside me in the bed. My beloved husband was sleeping like a child. I kissed him on the lips, he woke up, and I greeted him.

He looked at me passionately, "I love you even more than you think; it is quite difficult to find any lady at your age to keep her virginity till her wedding night. I am proud of you, my love," he said to me.

We kissed till we made love again and then slept off again.

We indulged in a languid afternoon, sleeping in until the warmth of the sun had fully filled our room. Karl, ever the thoughtful partner, stirred first, rising from bed with a gentle stretch. He padded softly to the kitchen, where the aroma of freshly toasted bread soon wafted through the air, teasing my senses and building my anticipation. Returning to our bedroom, he presented me with a tray bearing a simple yet satisfying breakfast: crispy toast, soft bread, and a cold glass of milk. I savoured each bite, feeling pampered and cared for. As we lingered over our meal, we began to ready ourselves for the day, taking our time to freshen up and even sharing a leisurely bath together. The gentle lapping of the water against our skin, combined with the warmth of each other's company, created a sense of deep relaxation and contentment. The rest of the day unfolded at a similarly tranquil pace, with laughter and conversation flowing easily between us.

Three days after the wedding, we felt rejuvenated and eager to reconnect with our loved ones, so we embarked on a series of visits to our parents and close friends, eager to share our joy with them. A week after our wedding, Terry, Jamila, Titi, and Shun travelled back to China. Mama stayed back for some time.

Our wedding became the buzz of the town for more than three months. Our photos appeared in numerous magazines and on billboards, and we received requests for interviews. We became celebrities, not just in Nigeria but also in China. We went on a honeymoon in Hawaii. Karl took me on a date to one of the best restaurants in Hawaii. I enjoyed my honeymoon. We came back home after three months. I poured wine into two glasses and carried them outside to our cozy mini lounge, where Karl was engrossed in a basketball match on his iPad. I handed him a glass, and he smiled in appreciation, taking a moment to acknowledge my thoughtful gesture.

"Thank you love," he said.

I sat down close to him and looked into his eyes. I kissed him passionately.

"You are the best thing that has ever happened to me. Thank you so much for everything. God will not stop blessing you, my dear husband," I said.

Karl pulled me closer to him. I rested my head on his chest.

"Thanks for sticking to me, not minding the trials and challenges we have been through. I promise to love you eternally. We will train our children in love and God's way," he replied.

"Oma, thank you for giving me such a treasure. I appreciate your love. I will never turn your love down, and by the grace of God Almighty, we will live happily till death do us part," he added.

I lifted my head off his chest, and he used his finger to tilt my face up to his. Then, he kissed me like he'd never kissed me before - like his life depended on it.

www.ingramcontent.com/pod-product-compliance
Lightning Source LLC
LaVergne TN
LVHW041107150826
845673LV00007B/1957

* 9 7 8 9 7 8 7 7 1 0 1 2 8 *